P9-DHJ-883

"Bring him here."

Caleb followed Tessa down the hallway to Sam's room and laid the child on his narrow bed. As he stood back, Tessa quickly removed Sam's socks and shoes. Caleb watched her motherly movements in silence. For just a moment, he could almost pretend Sam and Tessa were his and this was a natural everyday occurrence—putting their child to bed after a busy day of work. But it wasn't reality.

In silence, they stepped out of the room and Tessa pulled the door until it was slightly ajar.

"He's really worn out. *Danke* for being so kind to him," she whispered.

"You're *willkomm*," he returned.

They stood there in silence for several moments. Caleb didn't know what to say. It felt as if his heart was pounding in his ears. Once again, his mind was filled with questions he longed to ask her. Explanations he hoped might clarify what had happened so long ago and give him a transparent way to forgive her for what she'd done. But no answers were forthcoming and he wouldn't ask. Not again.

Leigh Bale is a *Publishers Weekly* bestselling author. She is the winner of the prestigious Golden Heart® Award and was a finalist for the Gayle Wilson Award of Excellence and the Booksellers' Best Award. The daughter of a retired US forest ranger, she holds a BA in history. Married in 1981 to the love of her life, Leigh and her professor husband have two children and two grandkids. You can reach her at leighbale.com.

Visit the Author Profile page at LoveInspired.com for more titles.

Her Forbidden
Amish Child

Leigh Bale

LOVE INSPIRED
INSPIRATIONAL ROMANCE

If you purchased this book without a cover you should be aware that this book is stolen property. It was reported as "unsold and destroyed" to the publisher, and neither the author nor the publisher has received any payment for this "stripped book."

LOVE INSPIRED®

INSPIRATIONAL ROMANCE

ISBN-13: 978-1-335-58506-6

Her Forbidden Amish Child

Copyright © 2022 by Lora Lee Bale

All rights reserved. No part of this book may be used or reproduced in any manner whatsoever without written permission except in the case of brief quotations embodied in critical articles and reviews.

This is a work of fiction. Names, characters, places and incidents are either the product of the author's imagination or are used fictitiously. Any resemblance to actual persons, living or dead, businesses, companies, events or locales is entirely coincidental.

For questions and comments about the quality of this book, please contact us at CustomerService@Harlequin.com.

Love Inspired
22 Adelaide St. West, 41st Floor
Toronto, Ontario M5H 4E3, Canada
www.LoveInspired.com

Printed in U.S.A.

Recycling programs for this product may not exist in your area.

Jesus saith unto him, If I will that he tarry till I come, what is that to thee? follow thou me.
—*John* 21:22

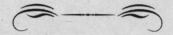

Chapter One

This was a big mistake. Huge! But what other choice did she have? Tessa Miller stared at the double glass doors at Yoder's Diner and took a deep, settling breath. If ever she'd had a bad idea, this was it. She knew it deep in her gut. But right now, she was out of options.

Standing on the front boardwalk, she trembled in spite of the warm June weather. Afternoon sunshine gleamed against the black asphalt running down Main Street. Bright marigolds and purple petunias grew in a large clay pot outside the front doors. A gentle breeze brought the pungent scent of sage. But these things were just distractions. There was no putting off the inevitable.

Turning the doorknob, she stepped inside. A gust of air-conditioning struck her in the face, cooling her hot cheeks. Though the Amish had no electricity in their homes, many of them did have it in their shops, stores and restaurants. The little bell over the door tinkled to herald her arrival. With her first inhale, she caught the pleasant aromas of fresh-baked bread and roast chicken.

"Be right with you," a cheery voice called from the opposite side of the diner.

Doris Yoder was sliding two plates of food onto a table for an older *Englisch* man and woman…the only customers Tessa could see. Tourists or locals, Tessa didn't recognize them. Not odd, since the Amish kept to themselves.

At church two days earlier, Doris had promised Tessa a waitressing job. But at three o'clock on a Tuesday afternoon, the diner wasn't busy. Since Tessa would be working here, she filed that bit of information away in her brain. Yoder's was one of two restaurants in the sleepy farming town of Riverton, Colorado. With a population of fewer than five thousand people, that was all the economy could support here. No doubt business would pick up as they got closer to the supper hour.

Twining her hands together to keep them from shaking, Tessa waited patiently for Doris to join her. Her heart pounded like a bass drum, and she shifted her weight, trying to remain calm as she looked around.

Though she'd been here many times years earlier, there were subtle changes. A fresh coat of gray paint adorned the walls, which held decorative wooden shelves that supported old-fashioned water pitchers, oil lamps and long-handled spoons. Quaint and homey. A nice, *familye* place to have breakfast, lunch or dinner.

A long barrier at the front counter had been set up to shield the mechanical cash register from easy theft. Behind that, a huge blackboard menu hung on the far wall. To one side, a glass refrigerator case gleamed with an array of homemade pies, cupcakes, breads and other treats. Though Doris made plenty of bread and rolls for the diner, Tessa knew other Amish women in their community provided some baked goods in return for a small commission.

A wide cutout showed a glimpse into the kitchen, where the cook prepared the meals. Warming lamps lined a narrow cubby where plates of food waited until Doris could shuttle them to the hungry customers.

Tessa counted twenty-five square tables, covered with red-and-white-checkered cloths and accompanying wooden chairs, where the patrons ate their meals. Yoder's Diner was simple, clean and tidy. A charming place to work. But that wasn't the problem. Doris had said the job was Tessa's, but she'd be forced to work every day with Caleb Yoder, the owner, and cook for the diner. And working for the man she'd once loved— and whose heart she'd broken—wouldn't be easy. Not for either of them.

She turned, thinking she should leave. Right now. While she still had the chance.

"Tessa! *Ach*, I'm so glad you came."

Too late! She jerked her head to the side. Doris, Caleb's mother, stood in front of the baked goods. Glancing at Tessa, the woman slid two menus into a holder by the cash register. She spoke in *Deitsch*, the German dialect their Amish people used among themselves.

Gathering her courage, Tessa licked her dry lips and reminded herself of her goal. She needed this job. Badly. To provide for her four-year-old son, Samuel. If not for him, she wouldn't be here. Not ever again.

"*Komm!* I'll take you back to Caleb. I told him our new waitress was coming in to meet him today. He's happy I found a *gut* worker to wait tables for us." Doris bustled over to her, wiping her hands on a black apron covering her long lavender dress.

At the age of sixty-four, Doris was rather matronly, with a jovial smile and gray-streaked hair she wore tucked beneath her starched white prayer *kapp*. She was the mother of nine children, and Caleb was the youngest. Wearing the standard clothes of an Amish woman, she was dressed much like Tessa, with plain black stockings and practical black shoes.

She nodded, forcing herself to smile. "Are you sure he won't mind me working here?" Tessa tossed a skeptical glance toward the kitchen, knowing Caleb must be back there somewhere.

Doris waved a hand in the air. "Of course not. We need the help, and you need a job. Let's go talk to him."

Pulling on Tessa's arm, Doris propelled her toward the kitchen. Absolute panic clawed at Tessa's throat when she thought about talking to Caleb again. Though she saw him regularly at church on Sundays and at other gatherings hosted by their Amish community, that was different. That was from far across the room, where she was insulated by other people and never needed to speak directly with him. But today, she'd be right next to him as she asked him for a job. And though Doris had said it was hers, Tessa had doubts.

"Caleb!" Doris called. "That new waitress I told you about is here. And she's an experienced baker, too. She'll be perfect for us."

That new waitress? Oh, no! A sinking feeling settled in Tessa's stomach. Had Doris not told Caleb it was her? Oh, dear. This might not be good.

Holding an empty frying pan, Caleb stepped into the doorway, his tall frame filling the threshold. Tessa blinked and gazed up at his solemn face, forcing herself not to bolt.

He wore the simple black shoes and broadfall pants that all their Amish men wore. Beneath his pristine blue cook's apron, his black suspenders crossed his white chambray shirt. He'd rolled the long sleeves up on his muscular arms, no doubt so he could work and wash dishes. At first sight of her, his mouth hardened and his dark eyes narrowed. His lips twitched in that unique manner she recognized so well from their childhood. He wasn't pleased to see her. No, not at all.

His black hair was slicked back on his head in tidy perfection. Since their men normally wore it slightly long and shaggy, she figured he must keep it cut short for his profession. That would undoubtedly please any health inspectors who might pay a surprise visit to the restaurant. Without speaking, he set the pan aside with a little thump. His blunt chin looked hard as granite, and he appeared so formidable standing there as he folded his arms.

So intimidating.

"*You* are the new waitress?" he asked, his low voice filled with disapproval, as if he couldn't believe her audacity in coming here.

Tessa pressed the tip of her tongue against her upper lip and nodded. "Um, your *mudder* said you were hiring. She…she said I could have the job."

Okay, not too forceful, but she was desperate

enough to try and push the issue. She needed this job. It wouldn't be a huge salary, but the real blessing was the small, two-bedroom apartment sitting upstairs from the restaurant. The stairs at the side of the building offered a private entrance. According to Doris, the apartment was vacant, and Tessa and Sam could move in today. It wasn't fancy, but was furnished and included a small kitchenette, bathroom and living area…all that Tessa and Sam needed.

Finally, she could live independently. Finally, she'd have a place of her own. If she had to return to live with her older brother and his wife and children, she'd spend the rest of her life feeling like an unwanted burden. Like an outsider in her own home. And over time, she had no doubt that would decay her heart. She couldn't accept that the rest of her life would be spent being dependent on them. She had to make it on her own. She must!

"Who would look after Sam while you're working?" Caleb asked about her son.

"*Ach*, I'll do that," Doris said. "He'll stay with me in the back office while I work on our accounts. He can play and read or lie down on the cot if he gets tired. And sometimes, I'll take him to our farm."

Doubt filled Caleb's eyes. But the fact that he'd even mentioned her son impressed Tessa. Now they just needed him to agree.

The bell at the front door tinkled, notifying them that someone had come inside.

"*Ach*, there's another customer. I'll leave you with Caleb. He can tell you all about your new job," Doris said, her voice sounding firm as she tossed an insistent nod at her son. With no more than a backward glance, the woman disappeared into the outer room, leaving Tessa alone with Caleb.

He stared at her for several moments, then raked a hand through his hair. Another unique gesture she recognized that showed his frustration. She could tell he didn't like this situation at all.

"What's your work experience? Can you wait on customers? Have you even been a waitress before?" he asked.

"*Ne*, but you know I've worked on my *bruder*'s farm all my life," she said.

"Can you cook and bake bread?" He stepped back into the kitchen before she could answer.

She followed him. "You know I can."

Why was he asking such silly questions? He'd known her since she was twelve years old. He knew she could cook and bake and that she had an excellent work ethic.

He looked through the cutout to the diner, and she realized he was paying attention to what was going on with his customers. Doris had seated two *Englisch* women at a table and offered them menus and ice water. Tessa knew instinctively that Caleb had a few more minutes before Doris delivered their food order for him to prepare.

"What about waitressing? Have you ever done that?" Caleb asked.

She shook her head. "*Ne*, not in a formal capacity. But I've cooked and served food to dozens of people at our church gatherings. I know how to wait on people. You know all of this, Caleb."

He jerked his head toward her, seeming surprised that she'd called him by name. There'd been a time when she'd said his name so tenderly, so sweetly, with love ringing in her voice. Now, she said his name with a tinge of exasperation.

His mouth pursed and his expression turned to one of begrudging acquiescence. That was when Tessa knew he would do whatever his mother wanted. Thankfully, Doris had always loved her. They'd all thought she and Caleb would marry one day. But that was before she'd messed up her life with her foolish actions. She would have been Doris's daughter-in-law by now. Sam should have been Caleb's son. But after what Tessa had done, she'd expected the woman to disapprove of her. Yet Doris had shown her an increase in love. She'd been so forgiving. Doris had even gone out of her way to seek Tessa out and ask if she'd like to work at the diner. It seemed they were having trouble acquiring extra help. And Tessa had jumped at the offer.

"I know you can cook and serve food, but waitressing is different. You'll need to work the ice cream machine and coffee makers. You'll have to make change when the customers pay their bills. Have you ever worked a cash register?" he asked.

"*Ne*, but I can make change. I was always *gut* at math. I can learn how to work the machines, too. I can do this job well, if you'll just give me a chance," she said.

"I don't know…"

She caught a hint of uncertainty in his voice—as

well as a healthy dose of resentment. He didn't want her here. And she couldn't blame him.

She'd given birth out of wedlock. By *Englisch* standards, that wasn't so bad. But being Amish, it was unconscionable. Because Caleb wasn't the father and she'd remained unmarried.

She'd been barely eighteen years old at the time, the same age as Caleb. They'd been engaged to wed. It was their *rumspringa*, that rite of passage during adolescence when Amish teenagers experience freedom of choice without the rules of their church *Ordnung* to hold them back. Against Caleb's wishes, Tessa had gone to Denver with an *Englisch* girlfriend. Thinking it harmless enough, she'd attended a house party among strangers, even enjoying her first glass of wine. Soon afterward, she felt dizzy and lost consciousness. Now, she had vague memories, but after she passed out, nothing was clear in her mind. The next morning, she awoke confused, her body bruised, her clothes torn. Realizing someone had spiked her drink, she'd returned to her *familye* posthaste. Feeling responsible, it had been easy to hide her injuries beneath the long sleeves of her modest dresses. She'd known something bad had happened to her that night, but she was too young and naive to understand the implications.

Within three months, she discovered she was pregnant with her little son, Samuel. No one but Tessa knew she'd been violated that night. Because the Amish were pacifists and kept to themselves, they only involved the *Englisch* authorities as a last resort. She never went to the police. Never told another living soul.

To this day, she felt ashamed and responsible for

what happened to her. But that wasn't the worst part. No one knew the identity of her child's father. Not even her. Tessa never told Caleb or even her own parents what had happened. Because, honestly, she didn't know. And though she longed for a happy marriage and *familye* life of her own, she felt unworthy of them. She was damaged goods now. Though she was single, no one asked her out. No decent Amish man wanted her anymore.

Caleb was rightfully angry with her. Not once had they discussed what had happened. After she returned home, he'd sought her out and she'd broken off their engagement. But every time she looked at him, she saw the deep hurt and anger in his eyes. The confusion and resentment. She'd broken his heart. But telling him the truth would be too shameful, too painful for her. And so, she'd never offered an explanation. Nothing. Not even a proper reason for the breakup. But it had to be this way. Because Caleb deserved a better woman than she could ever be. He deserved a fresh start with someone who hadn't betrayed him with her foolish notions of seeing the world.

He deserved to be happy.

For now, Tessa must focus on raising her son and try to earn a living the best way she could. Because she couldn't return to live the rest of her life with her brother and his *familye*. Not even if it meant working for a man who hated her for what she'd done.

"I don't see how this will ever work," Caleb said.

He stared at Tessa, hardly able to look away. With prominent cheekbones, luminous skin and crystalline blue eyes, she was beyond pretty. Her blond hair was pulled back and covered by her white prayer *kapp*. But even in the modest, plain clothes of the Amish, she was gorgeous. Of course, he would never tell her that. The Amish shunned *Hochmut*, the pride of the world. Beauty wasn't important to them. And yet, he couldn't help staring.

Forcing himself to look away, he wondered why she was here. Why did she want to work for him? His mom never should have offered her the job. But Doris loved Tessa. She always had. Tessa had been close with his *familye* during their growing-up years. Caleb's father had adored her. So had Caleb. Maybe Doris could forgive Tessa for what she'd done to him, but he couldn't. Not without some explanation. And she'd never offered him one.

"I'll work hard for you," Tessa said.

"I'm sure you will. But why here? Why now?" he asked, his voice filled with suspicion.

"I need the job."

Her voice carried a hint of desperation, and he didn't understand.

"You have Sam to look after, and you live with your *bruder*. Isn't working on his farm enough for you?" he asked.

"*Ne*, Wayne has his own *familye* now. He and Grace have four growing *kinder* and another one on the way. Their farmhouse is quickly running out of room. They haven't said anything, but I can tell they would rather Sam and I…"

Left.

She didn't say the word out loud, but she didn't have

to. Wayne was a kind man, but he probably didn't cherish the idea of having his younger sister and her son living with him the rest of their lives. Wayne wanted her to leave and get a life of her own. And though it wasn't Caleb's business, that upset him. Because she needed help. She needed protection.

"Sam and I are in the way," Tessa said, confirming Caleb's thoughts.

Hmm. Caleb didn't like what he was hearing, but he understood. Tessa's parents had died several years earlier, before his own father passed away. Caleb didn't believe Wayne would ever ask Tessa to leave the farm where she'd been raised. It wasn't the Amish way. Even if they didn't like it, they always took care of their own. But she'd undoubtedly worn out her welcome. After five years, it was time for her to marry and get her own home. And that should have been with him. But who would marry her now? No one he could think of. At least, not among their single Amish men.

He thought about her and Sam living on their own and didn't like it one bit. Because they were members of his Amish community, Caleb attended church with them, and he knew her little boy well. A delightful, intelligent child. Caleb would have loved to have a son like Samuel. If Tessa was alone, who would look after them? Who would teach Sam to run a farm and become a good man of faith? Who would keep Tessa and her little boy safe?

"Please, Caleb. I need this job," she said again.

Please! Was she so desperate that she would resort to begging? There was no resentment in her voice. Just an edge of recklessness, and also a composed accep-

tance for things as they were. And though the tenets of
their faith dictated that anger was not of Jesus Christ,
her words made Caleb mad. Downright furious! After
the way she'd gotten herself caught with a child outside
of wedlock and tossed him aside, how could she now
stand here and coolly ask him for a job?

"I don't see how it would work," he repeated.

She looked away, as if mulling this over, but not before he caught the shimmer of tears in her eyes. Her
lips parted a couple of times, as if she wanted to say
something more. But she must have reconsidered, because she clamped her mouth tight and just looked at
him steadily.

"Are you going to give me the job or not?" she finally asked.

"Order up!"

Both of them jerked as Doris snapped an order into
the circular holder at the front counter. Grateful for the
distraction, Caleb stepped over and jerked it free, rip-
ping the paper in the process. He held the two pieces
together, reading his mom's scrawled handwriting. A
large chef's salad with ranch dressing and a cheese-
burger and fries with no onion or mayo.

Setting to work, Caleb brushed past Tessa and
reached inside the gas-powered fridge for a raw patty
and slice of American cheese. He slapped the beef onto
the hot grill, where it sizzled.

How could he let Tessa work here? If he said no,
everyone would think he was being a bully. His lack
of kindness would be all over the *Gmay*, their Amish
community, by tomorrow morning. The Amish grape-
vine was swift and sure. All his people would know

that he'd turned his back on one of their own. And then they would rehash the way Tessa had dumped him years earlier and given birth to another man's child out of wedlock, as if it was fresh news.

He let Tessa watch him prepare the food. If she was going to work here, she needed to understand that nothing took precedence over their customers. This diner was their livelihood, and he didn't have time for nonsense. Nor would he tolerate any games.

"Can I help?" she asked.

"*Ne*, I'll have to train you first."

Feeling grouchy, he reached for a bag of shredded lettuce and a handful of cooked ham and thin turkey slices for the salad. He didn't want to hire this woman. Didn't want to be anywhere near her. But with his mother pushing him, he had little choice. Because as much as Tessa needed a job, he needed the extra help.

After suffering a mild heart attack last month, Doris couldn't work as hard anymore. That was why Caleb had hired other women to bring baked goods to the restaurant for him to sell. *Mamm* must cut back on her hours. She needed rest.

Up until three weeks ago, *Mamm* had done all the baking for the restaurant as well as waiting on the tables. They had not only the diner to run but also a small farm with thirty acres of land not two blocks away. With cows to be milked twice a day, pigs and horses to be fed, and eggs to be gathered, they worked from sunup to sundown. The livestock supplied the diner with most of its dairy needs. Additionally, they had a large vegetable garden and fields he'd planted in hay last week. He'd done the labor in the evenings, after he closed the diner for the day. Sometimes, he worked in the dark, after the sun had gone down.

Caleb could handle the heavy workload. He was young and strong. But *Mamm* needed to cut back on her assignments. Right now.

As the youngest of nine children, Caleb had inherited the restaurant and farm after his father died two years earlier. His older sisters and brothers had already married and moved away with livelihoods of their own. Because he'd never wed, his mom had stayed with him, so he wouldn't be alone. Though his days were long, Caleb didn't mind the work. It took his mind off the fact that he had no wife and *familye* to share his life with. It helped him forget Tessa and her betrayal. But he was worried about his mother. *Mamm* couldn't keep up the frantic pace anymore. Though they'd asked everyone they could think of within their church congregation if they'd like the job, they'd come up empty.

Caleb glanced toward Tessa. She stood beside the sink, out of his way. The rush of water drew his attention, and he saw that she was lathering her hands with a bar of *Mamm*'s homemade soap. Was she planning to help him right now?

As he sliced tomatoes and hard-boiled eggs, he felt awkward beneath her gaze. She was the last person he wanted to hire. But with a big catering contract for a town fund-raiser next week, he needed extra help. They could hire *Englisch* girls to wait tables, but that wasn't to his liking, either. Though he did business with the *Englisch* on a daily basis, the Amish kept to themselves. *Englischers* didn't understand their unique ways, and Caleb didn't want to explain things that were normal to him but might seem odd to someone who wasn't Amish. But maybe that was preferable to working with the woman he'd once loved and longed to marry and now couldn't forgive no matter how hard he tried.

He flipped the burger patty and shook a little salt onto it, then reached for the sesame seed buns. The package was right in front of his nose. Anticipating his movements, Tessa handed it to him. As he pulled out a bun, he was distracted and not paying attention. He backed into the gas stove, and the long strings to his apron caught fire.

"Caleb! Look out!" Tessa called.

He gasped. Before he could react, he found his front and side drenched as she threw a pitcher of water on him. Though the flames had been effectively doused before any harm could be done, he was almost completely soaked from his chest to his ankles.

"What happened?" Doris ran into the room and stood gaping with shock.

"He…he was on fire," Tessa exclaimed.

Caleb couldn't move. He felt frozen in place, holding his arms open by his sides, his hands splayed as he stared down at himself. All he could do was stand there in shock as he dripped on the floor. Though he now needed to change his clothes, he realized Tessa's quick thinking had undoubtedly saved him from a nasty burn.

"Are you *allrecht*?" Doris asked, taking a step closer.

Recovering his senses, he made a soothing motion

with his hands. "*Ja*, I'm *allrecht*. No harm done. But I need to go *heemet* and change out of these wet clothes."

Tessa handed him a dish towel. He took it and wiped the front of his shirt. She reached for the mop and bucket sitting behind the door and started to sop up the puddle on the floor.

Mamm grabbed the metal spatula and lifted the burger patty off the grill before sliding it onto the bun.

"You run *heemet* and change," *Mamm* said. "Tessa and I will look after the diner while you're gone. And later this evening, after we've closed up, you can drive out to her *bruder*'s farm and help her and Sam move their belongings into the apartment upstairs."

Caleb blinked. "They're going to be living here, too?"

Oh, this just kept getting better and better. And not in a good way!

"Of course! They've got to have a place to live. The apartment is vacant and handy to the restaurant. It'll be perfect for them," *Mamm* said.

Caleb shifted his weight, his woolen socks feeling damp in his shoes. His soggy pants and shirt clung to his body in a sodden mass. He felt uncomfortable and irritable. But as he faced *Mamm*'s dogged determination, he could offer no reasonable argument why they shouldn't hire Tessa to start work immediately.

"I… I don't want to cause trouble," Tessa said.

She looked so small and defenseless, standing there with her hands gripping the mop handle. The deep blue of her plain Amish dress almost exactly matched her cerulean eyes. Though he knew she worked in the sunshine on her brother's farm, her complexion seemed pale and gaunt today. Her white apron and prayer *kapp* gave her a guileless, endearing look. But she wasn't innocent. She wasn't naive. And she wasn't his. Not anymore.

"You're not causing trouble. Not at all," *Mamm* exclaimed.

Caleb heaved a heavy sigh of annoyance. He couldn't fight his mother. Not when she still wasn't feeling well. Without another waitress, the heavy burden on his mother could prove fatal. He must hire more help. But never in his wildest dreams had he thought it would be Tessa.

"We'll see how it works out. I'll give you a trial period of three months," he heard himself say.

There. That was good. If things didn't go well, no one could blame him. And three months would give him time to find someone else. Maybe one of the teenaged Amish daughters who had just finished their schooling. But it was planting time, and all those girls were needed on their families' farms. For now, Caleb was stuck with Tessa. There was no one else. But maybe in the fall, after harvest was over, he could find someone else.

Tessa nodded, a tight smile curving her full lips. "*Ja*, that's all I can ask. But you won't regret it. I promise."

He regretted it already. Her words weren't worth anything to him. She'd promised to love and marry him, and look how that had turned out. He didn't trust her. Not now. And yet, she looked so relieved that he realized how much this job meant to her. He had no doubt she'd work hard. What he doubted was his own ability to be near her every day and not have his heart shredded again and again.

"I'll be back." Turning, he stepped out the back door into the shade-covered alleyway and trudged toward his waiting horse and buggy. The animal stood beneath a canopy he'd installed to keep the beast protected from the sun and rain. A small water trough sat nearby. He quickly harnessed the animal to the buggy.

The ride to his farm took less than ten minutes. They always brought a horse in the morning because of all the food they had to carry from their farm. Just now, he would have walked home, but didn't want to deal with curious stares from people noticing his soggy demeanor.

As he changed his clothes and hurried back to the diner, Caleb thought about the past. He was Amish and never wanted to venture outside his peaceful, orderly world. He loved the quiet calm of Riverton. Never had he been overly curious about *Englisch* life like Tessa was. Besides her, his Amish faith was all he'd ever wanted. That and a brood of children to love. But against his wishes, she'd taken off with a friend and gone to Denver. He'd asked her not to go. His father had been ailing at the time and needed his help at the restaurant. So, she'd gone without him. And when she'd returned four days later, he'd expected her to come visit him. To be excited as she told him all about her adventures among the *Englisch*. But she never came. Four days later, he went to her father's farm, seeking her out. She'd said nothing except that she no longer wanted to marry him. When he'd asked her why, she told him she didn't love him anymore. That they weren't compatible. Which was utterly ridiculous. She'd refused to say any more, but he knew something was wrong. Something big.

He'd thought his heart had broken in two. After that, he saw her at church, but she no longer looked for him. No longer sought him out or wanted to chat. Instead, she seemed overly quiet, withdrawn and…

Deeply saddened.

At first, Caleb thought he'd done something wrong. Maybe Tessa was angry with him for not going with her to Denver. He'd thought it would blow over and they'd get back together. But three months later, he'd learned she was expecting a baby. He'd found out from his mother, who'd heard it from another woman in their *Gmay.*

Caleb could hardly believe the news. Only a few months before, they'd been crazy in love and planning their marriage. Now, she was having another man's child!

How could she do this to him? For years, he'd used restraint and shown her respect. Never would he have ill-used her. And here she'd gone off to Denver and gotten herself pregnant. Out of wedlock. With some stranger she refused to name!

Before he'd died, Caleb's dad had bluntly asked Caleb if he was the father of Tessa's baby. Knowing that wasn't possible, Caleb had denied it vehemently. But he could see the questioning looks thrown his way at church. His people wondered about him. They asked why he wouldn't marry her and what had happened to cause such a rift between them. And the sad part was, he didn't know. All he could figure was she'd fallen head over heels in love with someone else. Which meant she truly didn't love Caleb anymore. And that hurt most of all.

Once Tessa's baby was born and the father never showed up to claim them, Caleb approached her and offered to marry her. He was willing to forgive and forget. He wanted to give her child a name. Wanted their life to be like it was, before her betrayal. But she'd refused. He asked what had happened in Denver, but she wouldn't tell him a thing. And over the past four years, they'd become like strangers. He'd stood back and watched as she raised her son without a father. Without a husband. She seemed so aloof and cold, with no real friends. Not anymore. None of their eligible Amish men wanted to date her now. And though Caleb's mind was tortured by questions he longed to ask, he didn't know what to think. All he'd ever wanted was a wife and *familye* of his own.

All he'd ever wanted was Tessa.

Now, he felt locked in limbo. He couldn't move forward, but he couldn't go back, either. He was stuck in a private torture filled with confusion, anger, heartache and grief. He couldn't bring himself to marry another young woman from their *Gmay*, yet he didn't want Tessa anymore, either. Not when she didn't love him. Not when he couldn't trust her.

Now, she'd be working at the diner every day. Waiting on tables, baking, cleaning, helping with their chores. *Mamm* seemed so happy, her voice filled with a buoyancy Caleb hadn't heard since before his father's death. He didn't want *Mamm* upset. Not with her heart condition. Nor did he want to help Tessa move into the apartment above the diner later this evening. But it appeared his mother and her poor health wasn't giving him a choice.

Chapter Two

"*Guder owed*, Wayne," Caleb called to Tessa's brother.

Caleb pulled the horse and wagon to a halt beside the white frame farmhouse where Tessa had been raised. Her older brother, Wayne, stood in the middle of the graveled driveway, holding a bucket of grain. It was just after eight o'clock, and the man was undoubtedly doing his evening chores. Seeing Caleb, Wayne placed the bucket on the back porch and came to greet him. Caleb set the brake and hopped down.

The air smelled of something good cooking for supper. Two young children stood near the corrals, feeding the pigs and chickens. Flower beds lined the edge of the house, filled with an assortment of yellow and orange marigolds. Grace, Wayne's wife, waved at them from where she was pulling clean sheets off the clothesline. Shielding her eyes from the evening sun, she rested one hand against her rounding abdomen. Caleb figured she must be about six months along with her fifth child.

"You here to get Tessa and the boy?" Wayne asked.

"*Ja,*" Caleb said.

"*Gut!* You'll look after them, won't you?"

"Sure." Caleb nodded, knowing this was not what he'd signed up for. The last thing he wanted was to look out for his old flame and her illegitimate—but adorable—son.

Grace picked up her laundry basket and sauntered over to them. She stumbled in the process, and Wayne shot out his arms to steady her. Though the Amish rarely showed physical signs of affection, he pulled her in close against his side.

"Are you *allrecht*?" he asked gently.

She smiled up at him, her eyes filled with devotion. "*Ja,* I'm fine."

A searing pain of jealousy blazed through Caleb's chest. How he envied the love and respect Wayne and Grace shared. But coveting what others had, even their happy relationship, went against the tenets of his faith, so he pushed such feelings aside as he focused on the task at hand.

"You're here to get Tessa and Sam?" Grace asked him.

He nodded. "*Ja,* she'll be living and working at the diner now. My *mudder* made all the arrangements."

"Do you plan to marry her?" Wayne asked.

Caleb blinked at such frank candor, then shook his head. "*Ne,* she just wants a job."

A man of about thirty-two years of age, Wayne tugged on the brim of his straw hat and glanced at the house and frowned. Caleb was certain that his own father had talked to Tessa's dad before the two men had died. No doubt Wayne knew Caleb was not Sam's father.

"She doesn't have to go, you know. We didn't ask her to leave," Wayne said, his voice tinged with a bit of guilt.

"*Ne*, we would never do that. We love Tessa. And she's a great help with our *kinder*. She's always *willkomm* here," Grace added.

Caleb didn't respond. He told himself it wasn't his place. Though he'd known Wayne and Grace for years, Tessa's *familye* life was her business. The three of them stood there in silence for several moments.

Finally, Wayne released a heavy sigh. "I guess she feels like she's in the way."

Hmm. It sounded like Wayne and Grace were suffering from a dose of remorse. Maybe they hadn't asked Tessa to leave, but perhaps they hadn't asked her to stay, either. With a house full of kids, Caleb couldn't really blame them. Tessa was too beautiful to ever be an old maid, but her situation was rather unique. He felt sad that she might never wed. When he considered his own lack of marriage, he felt even worse. But there just wasn't anyone he was interested in. Maybe that would change later down the road, but not right now.

"I know she wants her own life now she's got Sam and you two aren't going to..."

Wayne didn't finish his statement, but he didn't have to. Caleb knew what the man was going to say—now that he and Tessa weren't going to marry. Caleb was glad everyone had finally figured that out. For the past five years, people in their congregation kept pushing him and Tessa together, especially Bishop Yoder, the leader of their *Gmay*. The bishop wasn't related to Caleb, though they had the same last name. They just didn't get it. Caleb and Tessa were through. Finished. Done.

"Maybe it's for the best that she goes," Wayne continued. "She should have been with you all along. Maybe this will make things right between you two. Maybe you can make a new start."

No, that wasn't going to happen. But Caleb didn't know how to respond. This was the most Wayne had ever said to him about the issue. All Caleb could do was stand there with his thumbs slung around his black suspenders and stare at the house. Though his mind was filled with raw emotions, he had no words right now. There would be no new starts for him and Tessa. Nothing would ever be right between them again.

"We're ready!"

Caleb looked up and saw her coming down the back porch steps, struggling with a heavy box.

Hurrying to her side, he scooped the box into his arms and slid it into the back of the wagon.

"Do you have much stuff to pack up?" he asked, refusing to meet her eyes.

"Not too much." She beckoned to him, and he followed her into the house.

Wayne and Grace remained outside.

Perhaps five boxes and one worn suitcase were stacked in a corner of the kitchen. Not much indeed. Thankfully, the apartment over the diner was furnished. *Mamm* was there right now, cleaning the place from stem to stern. Though Caleb had asked her to rest instead, she'd insisted, and he couldn't help worrying about her. He wanted Tessa and Sam to be comfortable, but he didn't like fretting over them, either.

"Sam! We're packing up to leave. Come and help," Tessa called to the back of the house.

The boy came running. He was a scrawny kid of just four years, with a thatch of sand-colored hair falling over his forehead, a guileless smile and big brown eyes that didn't match his mother's at all. A constant reminder that the boy must look a lot like his father. Whoever that was.

"Hi, Caleb!" the child called.

"Hallo!" Caleb couldn't resist smiling in greeting. After all, they knew each other from church and other gatherings. And what had happened in the past wasn't this innocent boy's fault.

Sam immediately tried to pick up a box, grunting as he struggled to heft its weight.

Tessa laughed and ruffled the boy's hair. "I'm afraid that's too heavy for you, *sohn*. Why don't you carry my knitting instead?"

She handed him a wicker basket filled with skeins of colorful yarn.

"Danke, Mammi," Sam said, smiling happily.

"But don't drop it. I don't want the yarn to get dirty," she warned as he slipped outside.

"I won't," he called as the screen door clapped closed behind him.

Caleb picked up two boxes at a time. "Is this everything?"

She nodded. *"Ja*, it's all I have in the world, except for Sam. But it's enough."

There was no resentment in her words. She picked up the suitcase and held the door open for him as he stepped out on the back porch.

Looking up, she glanced at the horse and wagon. "Didn't Doris *komm* with you?"

"*Ne*, she's back at the diner, cleaning your apartment," he said.

"*Ach, ne!* She should be resting. I can clean later."

She sounded as outraged as he felt, and he liked her concern for his mother. Everyone in their *Gmay* knew about Doris's heart condition. For a week after her heart attack, members of their congregation had brought meals in and given their house a thorough cleaning, in spite of the fact that Caleb was a proficient cook and ran a farm and restaurant. They all loved Doris. Caleb figured the food and cleaning was just their way of showing it.

He slid the two boxes into the wagon, then took the suitcase from Tessa's hands and stashed it inside, too. As he did so, their fingers brushed together, and he jerked back in surprise. He quickly turned away, hoping she wouldn't see how her touch impacted him. He could still feel the warmth of her skin against his fingertips and realized it was the first time he'd touched her in almost five years.

Without a word, he headed back to the house to retrieve another load. Tessa followed, and he could feel her eyes boring a hole in his back. They worked in silence, and he was satisfied with that. But a new tension had sprung up between them. The old physical attraction was still there. He could feel it every time she was near. But an awareness of all they'd lost lay between them like a raging river of dark, murky water.

Once they were loaded, Tessa stowed a wicker basket with a lid in the front seat as Grace called her children to come say goodbye. The kids stood in a stair-step lineup, their sweet faces smiling as Tessa hugged each one in turn.

"I love you," she said.

They returned the sentiment, hugging Sam as well. Then, Tessa faced Grace and Wayne. As they embraced, Caleb saw true affection in their eyes. No one had asked Tessa to leave, and he couldn't help wondering why she felt compelled to go. Did she truly want to be on her own? Or was there something more going on that he didn't understand?

"I'll see you at church on Sunday," Tessa said.

"*Ach*, of course you will. We'll be seeing lots of each other. It's not as if you're moving far away," Wayne said.

The man stood back as Tessa approached the wagon. Caleb was mildly surprised when Sam reached his arms out to him so he could swing the boy up onto the high seat. Then he took Tessa's elbow to stabilize her as she climbed on board.

Once she was settled, her basket beside her feet, she turned and waved to her *familye*. "*Mach's gut!*"

"*Seh dich, eich, wider!*" Grace called goodbye.

Caleb rounded the wagon and climbed into the driver's seat. Taking the leather leads into his hands, he released the brake and clicked to the horse. The wagon rattled forward, and they were off.

For a time, Wayne and Grace's children chased after

them, waving and hollering farewells. But once they reached the turnoff to the county road, the kids fell back and returned to their farm chores. Caleb was now truly alone with Tessa and Sam.

As Caleb turned the horse and headed toward town, a deep sense of duty enveloped him. Even though he wasn't married to Tessa, she'd be working for him. She and Sam would be tenants living above his diner. Though he didn't like it, Caleb had given his word to Wayne and couldn't help feeling responsible for her.

No one spoke for a long time, and the ride became rather stilted. The tension returned. Tessa stared ahead, her slender spine ramrod straight. Only the plodding hooves of the horse striking pavement and Sam humming a mindless tune broke the silence.

The boy swung his short legs back and forth on the seat and talked about his new home.

"I hope it has a really tall tree. I want to climb so high," he said, lifting his spindly arms over his head for emphasis.

"There is one tree out front on the street, but I fear it's too small to hold your weight without breaking its branches. You won't be able to climb it for several more years," Caleb said.

Sam frowned thoughtfully. "*Ach*, then maybe *Mamm* can take me to the park sometime."

"*Ja*, we will do that," Tessa said.

Caleb didn't like that the boy had no farm or fields to run around in. The restaurant had no yard where the boy could play. Kids needed space, but there was none at the diner.

"You can *komm* to my farm," Caleb offered, regretting it instantly.

His farm had pigs, chickens and cows, so Sam could learn to milk and raise crops. But who would teach the boy? Sam wasn't his child. And yet, Caleb couldn't help wishing he was. If Tessa hadn't run off and gotten herself into trouble, they would have married and this little boy would have belonged to him.

The boy kept chatting away, which eased some of Caleb's apprehension. And for a few moments, he let himself pretend this was his *familye* and he was driving them home after visiting relatives. Then, Caleb remembered who Tessa was and who he was and all the broken dreams between them.

Something hardened inside him. For a few minutes, he had let down his guard. But not again. Tessa had made her choices long ago, but she couldn't choose the consequences that followed. Sam wasn't Caleb's son. And Caleb was not going to be sucked into being hurt again. He wasn't Tessa's husband. He was just her boss, driving her to a new home so she could waitress for him at the diner. They would have a professional, working relationship and nothing more. And that was that.

Caleb was staring at her again. Tessa could feel his gaze like a leaden weight. Looking straight ahead, she tried to ignore him and his brooding eyes, but it wasn't easy.

She glanced his way and he jerked, gazing at the road. A flush of pink covered his face with embarrassment, and she almost laughed. He was trying so hard to ignore her, yet he couldn't. Nor could she disregard him. Not after all they'd shared together in the past. Not after the way she'd hurt him. But she must remember he was her new boss. She worked for him and nothing more.

A buzz of excitement filled her when she thought of having her own home. She loved Wayne and Grace, but now she could do things her way. She could feel strong and independent rather than being a burden. And yet, a feeling of dread overshadowed her, too. She and Sam would be all alone in the upstairs apartment. There'd be no strong man to reach something down off the top shelf or open a stubborn jar, and no yard or farm animals for Sam to play with. The busy Main Street out front of the restaurant prohibited the boy from going outdoors without supervision. But maybe she could take Caleb up on his offer and let Sam visit his farm now and then.

She was truly alone. Caleb and Doris were nearby, but not if she needed immediate help. Tessa was determined not to ask for their assistance any more than absolutely necessary. She was resolved to stand on her own two feet. Resigned to taking care of her son from now on. She told herself she didn't need a man in her life. She didn't need anyone to make her feel happy and secure. She was just fine by herself. And yet, she longed for so much more.

"I got a pet frog in that pond over there," Sam said, pointing to a small body of water on the outskirts of town.

"You do?" Caleb said in a conversational tone.

Tessa could tell Caleb liked Sam. But that wasn't

hard. Who wouldn't like a cute little four-year-old boy with a sweet disposition and perpetual smile on his face?

"*Ja, Onkel* Wayne took us fishing there once. I have to keep my frog in the pond 'cause *Mammi* won't let me have him in the house. She found him in my sock drawer once and that was it," the boy said, thrusting one hand into the air, as if he were throwing the frog away.

Caleb's lips twitched. For just a moment, Tessa thought he might laugh. But then he slapped the leads against the horse's back and it was gone.

"What's your frog's name?" Caleb asked.

"Homer," the boy said without hesitation.

"That's a *gut*, solid name," Caleb said.

If the moment had been different, Tessa might have laughed out loud and recounted how she'd first found the frog living in Sam's chest of drawers back at her brother's house. But she doubted Caleb wanted to hear such tales.

Sam startled her when he reached inside his shirt-front and pulled out a small brown sack. Without asking permission, he took out a snickerdoodle and bit into the soft cookie.

Tessa took the sack from him and looked inside, discovering a half dozen more cookies. "Where did you get this?"

"*Aent* Grace gave it to me. Since we aren't gonna be there for dessert, she said I could have one before my supper," the boy said.

They'd been so busy packing for the move, they hadn't eaten yet. Tessa had given Sam some buttered bread to tide him over, but apparently it wasn't enough. It seemed everyone at her brother's farm was out of sorts and running late this evening. Exhaling a quiet sigh, Tessa shook her head. Though she didn't feel upset, she kept hold of the sack so he wouldn't be tempted to eat more until he'd had his meal. "That was thoughtful of your *aent*. I hope you said *danke* to her."

"I did." Sam smiled happily as he munched on his treat.

After a few minutes, they entered town, and he tapped her shoulder. "*Mamm*, I'm awful hungry. What are we gonna eat for supper?"

"I have a jar of chicken soup and bread in my basket. I'll feed you just as soon as we empty our boxes from the wagon so Caleb can go *heemet*," she said.

"*Ach*, but I'm hungry now," the boy groaned.

Caleb pulled the wagon into the side alley and parked right in front of the tall stairs leading up to the apartment above. Without a word, he hopped out and sauntered around to lift Sam off his seat.

Tessa looked for a safe way down, but was forced to reach out and rest her hands on Caleb's muscular shoulders as he took hold of her waist with his hands. As he set her on her feet, the physical closeness caused her cheeks to heat up like road flares.

"*Danke,*" she spoke softly.

Their eyes clashed, then locked for just a moment. He nodded and turned away, going to the back of the wagon with Sam. Within minutes, they each had something to carry. Tessa trailed behind Caleb, holding tight to the handrail as she navigated the steep stairs up to her new home. At Caleb's urging, Sam opened the door and they stepped inside.

"*Ach!* You're here. *Willkomm* to your new *heemet*," Doris greeted them in the small living area.

Wearing a soiled apron, the older woman clutched the handle of a blue mop bucket and several dirty rags. She set them beside the door and stepped back. A vase of fresh field flowers sat in the middle of the tiny kitchen table. The apartment was small but spotlessly clean. No doubt Doris had worked hard, and Tessa could find no fault with the place.

"I just finished cleaning the gas-powered fridge. It's small, but should work well for you and Sam." Doris smiled at the boy and pulled him in close for a tight hug.

Since he was used to this grandmotherly woman, Sam tolerated the embrace. Caleb didn't say a word, just set the two boxes he was carrying on the floor.

"You're so kind, Doris. *Danke* for all you've done. But I hope you'll stop and rest now," Tessa said.

Doris waved a hand in the air. "Nonsense! I feel fine. Let me show you around. And then I'll help you put your things away. We've got work tomorrow, so you'll need everything put in order tonight."

Caleb frowned, but headed out the door for another load. Tessa and Sam followed Doris as she bustled down a narrow hallway.

"This room is yours, and the smaller room is for Sam. The beds aren't big, but I just made them up with clean sheets and blankets." Doris stood back and let Tessa peer inside.

"This is very nice," she said.

"This is my room? All by myself?" Sam asked, his voice filled with awe. Back at Wayne's farm, he'd shared a room with two other boys.

Doris smiled and leaned down to meet the boy's eyes. "*Ja*, it is just for you."

The boy smiled and immediately sprawled across the bed. He looked around with curiosity and seemed happy to be here.

They immediately set to work, carrying all the boxes upstairs. While Doris helped put things away, Caleb disappeared. Tessa figured he must be downstairs, checking on the diner. Twenty minutes later, he came inside carrying a tray laden with hot chicken-fried steak, mashed potatoes and gravy, string beans, and thick slices of apple pie.

He set the tray on the table. "Are you hungry? I figured we all needed something to eat."

How insightful. Yet, Tessa didn't want to accept anything more. Not from this man.

"Yum! I'm starving," Sam said, immediately pulling one of the wooden chairs back from the table and climbing up onto it as he gazed expectantly at the delicious food.

Doris joined the boy as she looked at Caleb. "*Danke, sohn.* I don't think any of us have eaten this evening."

"But I brought soup to feed Sam. You didn't need to go to all this trouble for us," Tessa objected in a half-hearted voice.

The food smelled delectable, and her stomach rumbled. With all their work, she'd lost track of time, and it was getting late. Plus, she was bone weary for some unknown reason. Perhaps it was all the packing and tension of moving to a new place—not to mention being near Caleb again.

"Your soup is in the fridge and you can eat it tomorrow. Tonight, let's eat this and go to bed. We've got a full day ahead of us," Doris said.

"Not you," Caleb warned. "You're going to rest tomorrow. You've worked hard enough today. The only reason I've allowed it is because I wasn't here to stop you. Except to get something to eat, I don't want to see you in the restaurant tomorrow. Not even once. You'll stay at home or in the back office, where you can sit and rest."

Doris stared at her son. "*Ach*, that's nonsense."

He met her gaze without wavering, his jaw locked hard as granite. Tessa knew that stubborn look. He wouldn't budge. Not on something as important as this. But Doris could be obstinate, too. Caleb was only trying to shield his mother, and Tessa liked his fierce protection of his *familye*.

Feeling a bit awkward, Tessa sat quietly as Caleb joined them at the head of the table. Following his lead, they blessed and consumed the food. Though he was a man, he could cook as well as any woman she knew. He sat no more than an arm's reach away. She could have touched him if she'd stretched out her hand.

When they finished, she stacked the dishes. She looked at Sam. "I'll get these washed up. Then I'll put you to bed, young man."

"I want Caleb to read me a story first," Sam said.

In unison, they all turned and stared at Caleb. Tessa was flabbergasted by the boy's request and wasn't sure what to think. Sam had known Caleb all his life, but the child didn't know, nor could he understand, the history between Caleb and his mother. The expression of unease on Caleb's face was very telling. Sam's request was something he would ask a father to do. Not Caleb. Not a man who could neither shun nor accept them.

"*Allrecht.* What do you want me to read?" Caleb asked.

Tessa exhaled a low sigh of relief or angst—she wasn't sure which. Maybe both.

"I'll show you." Sam took the man's hand and led him down the hall to his new bedroom.

Caleb trudged along willingly, and Tessa was once more impressed by his kindness to her son. She knew Sam would show him the assortment of children's books she'd unboxed and placed on his dresser no more than half an hour earlier.

With Sam occupied elsewhere, she quickly cleaned up the kitchen. Doris sat down on the sofa and soon lay back, snoring softly while Tessa emptied another box and stacked it with the others by the door to dispose of later. With Doris and Caleb's help, she'd put away all her few possessions in the closets and cupboards, and there was little left to do before she had to be at work at five thirty in the morning.

Catching the low sounds of Caleb's voice, she tiptoed to Sam's bedroom and listened from the hallway. Caleb was reading a cute story about a boy learning to tell the truth after he threw his ball and broke a window.

As he read the book, Caleb adapted his voice to each character in the story. Sam's startled gasps and thrilled giggles told her that he was enjoying himself. And when Caleb finished the book, he snapped it closed with finality.

"Will you read me another story? Please!" Sam pleaded.

"Another?" Caleb said. "I've already read three."

"I know, but you act out the stories. *Mamm* just reads them in her regular voice," Sam said.

Caleb chuckled. "*Ach*, I'll read you one more, but that's it. It's getting late and you need to sleep."

"Okay!" Sam sounded delighted, and Tessa could envision him settling back against his pillows for one more book.

She stood there, leaning against the wall as she listened intently. And when Caleb finished with a flourish, her son erupted into peals of laughter.

"*Ne*, don't tickle me, Caleb. Don't!" Sam cried in a voice that indicated that was exactly what he wanted Caleb to do.

Lifting a hand to her chest, Tessa didn't dare move. She could hardly breathe as tears stung her eyes. She'd never heard her son laugh like this. It was amazing, and she couldn't take it all in.

"It's time for prayers now. Can you kneel with me beside your bed?" Caleb asked softly.

"*Ja*," came Sam's obedient reply.

Tessa couldn't help peeking around the corner. Her son was dressed in his plain gray jammies, kneeling beside the big man as they both leaned their folded arms against the soft mattress. Their heads were bowed, their eyes closed in reverence. And as Caleb said the words, Sam repeated them, thanking *Gott* for all their blessings and asking that He watch over them.

As they finished, Tessa pulled back so they wouldn't catch her eavesdropping. Her eyes were damp, and she wiped away tears. In that moment, she caught a glimpse of how life might have been if she'd married Caleb. And in her heart of hearts, she mourned the fact that he wasn't Sam's father.

"Tessa? Are you *allrecht*?"

She whirled around and found Doris standing behind her.

"*Ja*, I'm fine. I, um, I just wanted to check on Sam," she said.

Okay, it was a pitiful excuse, she must admit. She hurried back to the living area, wiping her face as she went, hoping Doris didn't see how Caleb's time with her son impacted her. But when she looked up, Doris stood beside the kitchen table, gathering her purse and feather duster. Her eyes were crinkled with concern and a great deal of compassion.

"*Ach*, my dear. Everything is going to work out okay. You must believe in that and have faith," Doris said.

Faith was all she'd had for years now. That and Sam. But she sensed Doris was referring to Caleb. There was an undercurrent of meaning in Doris's words that Tessa didn't quite understand. There was no love between her and Caleb now. There never could be again.

Tessa forced herself to smile and nod, then busied herself with folding an afghan her mother had crocheted for her years earlier. As she laid it across the back of the sofa, Caleb joined them, his expression rather stoic. She hoped he had no idea she'd been listening to him reading stories and praying with her son. Hopefully, Doris wouldn't tattle on her, either.

"Sam's finally asleep," he said.

Good. No doubt her son was exhausted. He'd had a busy day, too.

"I'm taking my *mudder* home now. Will you be okay until morning?" he asked.

Tessa avoided his gaze. "*Ja*, we have everything we could ever need. *Danke* for your help. You've both been most kind."

Taking the mop and bucket from his mother's hands, Caleb opened the front door and waited for Doris to exit. As he closed the door behind them, he didn't look back at Tessa. She knew, because she watched to see if he would. And once they were gone, she bolted the door, then sat on the couch and stared at the wall. A myriad of emotions washed over her when she considered all that she'd missed out on. Marriage to a good man like Caleb. A home and *familye* of her own. It was her own fault. She never should have gone to Denver without Caleb. Because of one foolish mistake, she'd lost the love of her life, and she could never get him back.

Realizing what she'd done, her body trembled and her breath caught in her throat. A low, mournful cry rose upward in her chest. Long ago, she thought she was finished crying over this dilemma, but she was wrong. The pain never let up, never got easier. Burying her face in her hands, she leaned forward and rocked herself silently. Tears flooded her eyes and she wept.

Chapter Three

◆

At precisely five fifteen the next morning, Tessa tottered down the treacherous stairs leading from her apartment to the diner below. Holding the handrail, she carried her sleeping son in her other arm, a book bag slung over her shoulder. By Amish standards, the hour wasn't early. Back at her brother's farm, Tessa would have been up and milking cows by four o'clock. But she'd been filled with too much nervous energy to sleep well the night before and had to fight off a yawn.

At her knock, Doris met her at the back door and admitted her to the kitchen. Caleb was nowhere to be seen. A rattle of blinds out in the dining room told her he was probably there, getting the diner ready to open for the breakfast hour.

"I thought you weren't coming in today," Tessa whispered, so she wouldn't waken Sam.

Doris shrugged. "I'm not staying *heemet* and doing nothing all day. I need to be of use." She gazed lovingly at Sam. "*Ach*, the sweet dear. Bring him in here."

Tessa followed the woman to the back office, where

she laid Sam on the narrow cot that sat beside the metal desk. Dressed in his jammies, the child immediately curled onto the thin mattress, his closed eyes flickering once.

"Here are his clothes for later, when he wakes up. And some books, paper and colored pencils to entertain him." Tessa pulled the boy's shirt, suspenders and pants out of the bag and laid them on a corner of the bed. She put his socks inside his shoes and placed them on the floor.

"*Ja*, I'll take *gut* care of him. And you can pop in and see him anytime you like. Don't worry," Doris said.

Don't worry? Tessa was highly aware she was now officially a single working mother. And how would this impact her little son, being cooped up in this tiny office all day? But it couldn't be helped. She had to work and provide a living for them. They would both have to make the best of it.

"I worry about him not being on a farm anymore. How will he learn to milk cows and work the land?" Tessa spoke low and didn't think Doris heard her as the woman moved to the desk where she was reconciling the restaurant's accounts.

Leaning over her son, Tessa brushed her fingers through his silky hair and kissed his forehead. A sound came from behind her, and she turned. Caleb stood in the doorway, watching her. A scowl crinkled his forehead. Feeling awkward and embarrassed that he'd caught her with her guard down, she stood up straight and ran a hand over the front of her plain dress.

"Are you ready to start training?" he asked.

Before she could answer, Doris stood and squeezed her upper arm.

"*Ach*, go on, then. You'll do fine. I'll *komm* out to show you a few things once we have a customer to wait on," the woman said.

Caleb took a deep breath, as though he was going to object.

"Then, I'll take Sam *heemet* with me for a while. I promised Caleb I wouldn't work hard today," Doris hurried on.

Caleb nodded in approval. Without another word, he returned to the kitchen, and Tessa took a deep, settling breath. She didn't cherish the thought of working alone all day with a surly man. But knowing her son was happy and safe with Doris filled her with enormous relief. She could do this. She must have faith, in *Gott* and in herself. Returning Doris's smile, Tessa stepped forward into her new future.

The kitchen wasn't overly large, but it was tidy and clean, the walls painted a light gray color.

"Where would you like me to begin?" she asked as she straightened the blue apron and cape that covered her cream-colored dress...her new waitress uniform. Doris had provided it to her last night.

Ten large cartons of eggs sat on the counter. Caleb jerked open the refrigerator door and placed the eggs inside with a gallon of fresh cream. With stainless steel double doors, the fridge seemed huge. Tessa had never seen one this big, but figured the restaurant needed it to store enough food for its customers. Obviously, the dairy items had come from Caleb's farm. No doubt he'd gathered the eggs and skimmed the cream just that morning, before coming into work.

"We'll get to your training in a moment. But first, with *Mamm* out of commission, I could use some help on my farm. Do you think you can *komm* over later this evening, after we close the diner? It might be *gut* for Sam, too," he said.

Wow! This was a surprise. Maybe he'd overheard her comment. But she hadn't expected Caleb to think about her son. Sam needed to learn farmwork and mingle with livestock. At Caleb's place, the boy could run and have a little freedom after being stuck inside the restaurant all day.

"I'll pay you for the extra work," Caleb continued.

Hmm. Working on Caleb's farm in the evenings would be the perfect solution for her. But it would also mean spending more time with him.

"*Ja*, that would be *gut* for Sam. Would you like me to *komm* in the early mornings, too? I could gather the eggs and feed your pigs," she said.

He pushed the fridge door closed and stood straight. He stared at her with a slight frown for several moments, as if thinking this over. Then he shook his head.

"*Ne*, it'll still be dark that early in the morning, and I don't want you and the little *bu* out walking the streets alone. But you can take your evening meals here in the restaurant with *Mudder* and me, then ride over with us in our buggy. When we're finished with the chores, I'll bring you back *heemet*. That way, you and Sam will be safe."

His consideration impressed her. And yet, Caleb had always been kind and compassionate. It was in his nature. Since she didn't have a horse and buggy of her own, she appreciated him offering her a ride. And since she'd be working such long hours, taking nourishing meals here in the restaurant would help ease her workload and reduce her food expense, too.

"*Ja*, I can do that. *Danke*," she said.

"*Gut*. I'm glad that's settled." He stepped over to the gas grill and flipped it on, speaking over his shoulder. "We have the town's pool fund-raiser next week, so we'll be getting ready for that over the next few days."

She nodded in understanding. Everyone in the area knew the town was trying to build a swimming pool for their community. The city council had scheduled a big fund-raiser in the park. There would be a number of booths and a big auction. Though the Amish would never use the pool, they still tried to participate in community efforts and had donated several handmade quilts for the event. And the city had asked Caleb to provide one of the eatery booths.

"Part of your duties here at the restaurant is food prep, washing dishes and cleaning," he said. "But your main duty is to take orders and serve food to our customers. Nothing is more important than providing excellent customer service."

"What if I've got dirty dishes piling up to be washed?" she asked.

"Even then. If we have customers wanting service, the dishes must wait. Whatever our customers want, we'll try to give it to them—within reason. Nothing is more important than happy customers. Do you understand?" He glanced her way.

She nodded. "Don't worry. I'll take *gut* care of them."

He turned back to his task, reaching for a large package of bacon. Wielding a razor-sharp knife, he slit the package open and quickly laid the thick slices on the grill. While the bacon sizzled, he reached for an inventory list and a pencil. The air soon filled with the tantalizing aroma of breakfast.

"We open at six o'clock. Before that time, I expect you to turn on the lights in the dining room and fill all the condiment containers and the salt, pepper and sugar dispensers. Don't open the window blinds until right before you unlock the front door," he said as he made a few check marks on the paper.

He barely looked at her, sounding so sterile and professional. Though Tessa had known this man since they were kids, she'd never seen this business side to him. But since their livelihoods depended on the success of the diner, she couldn't blame him.

"Once they're filled, put the salt and pepper containers on each table. The ketchup containers go inside the fridge. You'll take one to the table when a customer needs it." He jutted his jaw to where big, unopened cans of ketchup and mustard, a plastic funnel, and two water pitchers—one filled with salt and one with pepper—sat waiting on a large tray.

"Okay." She stepped toward them.

"Be careful when you open the number ten cans. The lids are sharp as razors, and you could easily cut yourself," he said.

She nodded, grateful for the warning. After all, she'd never handled such enormous cans before.

Realizing she'd need a can opener, she almost asked him where it was kept, but didn't want to disturb him. Instead, she took the initiative and rattled around in the drawers, looking for the tool. Hearing the commotion, Caleb jerked his head up, his eyes filled with questions.

"Can opener?" she was forced to ask.

Again, he pointed, and she found what she sought. As she placed the tool on the first can, she felt jittery inside. She wasn't used to the heavy weight of the number ten can, and the opener slipped off, the can thumping against the counter. The opener slit the top of the lid just enough for the pressure to shoot a spray of ketchup directly into her left eye.

"Oh!" she cried, dropping the can and clasping her eye. The vinegar in the ketchup hurt.

"*Ach*, let me see." Caleb stood close in front of her, holding a damp dishcloth.

She removed her hands, but kept her eye closed. "It stings."

He wiped her eye several times, smoothing the ketchup off her face. His movements were so infinitely gentle until, finally, she was able to open her eye. She gazed up at him in wonder. His head was bowed low so he could look at her face. So close that she could feel the tickle of his breath against her cheek. He smelled like spearmint toothpaste. For several moments, she felt frozen in place. Unable to move. Unable to breathe. Then, he folded the damp rag into her hand.

"Is that better?" he asked.

"Um, *ja*, it's fine now." She blinked her eyes and moved away, eager to put some distance between them.

She picked up the opener to continue her chore, startled when he took it from her. Their fingers brushed together, and she jerked back, a bit stunned by the warmth of his skin against hers.

In quick succession, his strong hands manipulated the opener with ease as he cut the lids off the two cans and tossed them into the big garbage container by the door. Then he set the opener aside and stepped back to the grill, flipping the bacon strips as easily as he breathed air.

"Danke," she said, her voice a bit wobbly.

He turned away. "You're *willkomm*. Once you've finished your chore, come and see me for the next task."

"Ja, I will." She picked up the loaded tray and hurried out into the dining room. Her body trembled, and she wondered why the interaction with Caleb should affect her so much. Hopefully, working with him would get easier. But right now, she wondered how this could ever last. He'd given her three months to prove her worth, and she intended to make the best of it.

Out in the dining room, she set the tray on each table in turn and quickly undid the lids to the salt and pepper shakers. She inserted the funnel, filled the decanters to the top, then screwed the lids on tight. When that was finished, she went to the fridge, where she found smaller bottles of ketchup and mustard. She filled each one to the brim and wiped the bottles clean for good measure. The entire chore took her twenty minutes.

"Caleb, I've finished."

He stood at the vegetable prep area, slicing carrots, potatoes, celery and onions on a chopping block. Scooping the chunks of vegetables into his big hands, he dumped them into a large pot. Tessa was fast learning that everything was oversized in this diner, supposedly to feed numerous people. From the looks of the cubed raw chicken Caleb had already cut up and the big package of noodles sitting nearby, he was making homemade chicken noodle soup. Since they hadn't started serving breakfast yet, she figured the fresh meat and veggies would tenderize in time for the lunch hour.

He glanced at the clock. "*Gut!* Right on schedule. Now, check the two bathrooms. Refill the paper dispensers and sanitize the toilets and sinks. You'll find cleaning products inside the cabinet in the office. Wash your hands *gut* after you've finished."

"*Allrecht,*" she said, thinking that would give her a few moments to check on her son.

She hurried into the office, happy to see bright drafts of sunlight gleaming through the wide, open window. Sam was sitting on the cot fully dressed as Doris helped him put on his plain black shoes.

"*Mammi!*" the boy called and hopped down to fling his arms around her legs.

"*Guder mariye, liebchen.*" She leaned down and kissed his forehead.

"Can we go outside and play?" he asked.

She smiled, her heart filled with adoration as she caressed his sweet face. Though his creation had been fraught with brutality, she loved him dearly. In all the trauma of finding out she was pregnant, Sam was the one bright light in her lonely life.

"I'm afraid I have to work," she said, going to the cabinet for the cleaning supplies.

"Ahh!" he grouched.

"But we're going to Caleb's farm after we close the restaurant later tonight," she said.

"But I wanna go now," Sam said.

Doris smiled as she came to stand nearby and placed her hands on her matronly hips. "Don't worry, Sam. I'll take you there later this morning, after you've had your breakfast and I've finished the accounts. The doctor told me to go for a short walk each day, so this will be *gut* for me, too."

"Hooray!" Sam jumped up and down and clapped his little hands.

Tessa nodded at Doris. "*Danke*. That would be so nice of you. Now, I've got work to do."

As she hurried to the bathrooms with her rags, extra toilet paper and sanitizing spray, she thought this situation was good for all of them, if a bit awkward. If only she could reconcile her feelings toward Caleb. She sensed he didn't want her here. And more than ever, she was determined to work hard, learn her job and keep her distance so she had to speak with him as little as possible.

She was watching him. Again. Caleb could feel Tessa's eyes boring a hole in his back like an electric drill he'd seen in the hardware store once.

As he gave his pot of soup a quick stir, he glanced her way. She looked perfectly innocent, sitting at the worktable as she wrapped napkins around silverware and secured them with a band before placing them in a large basket for a quick grab once they got busy. Thankfully, it was a Tuesday, their least hectic day of the week. With his mother's help, Caleb should have time to give Tessa more training before she had to face a heavy rush of customers tomorrow.

"Is this enough?" She looked at him, indicating the tub, which was filled with sufficient napkins and silverware to last them two days.

She was a quick worker, he'd give her that.

"*Ja*, that's plenty." He glanced at the clock on the wall. It was two minutes before six.

"What do you want me to do next?" she asked.

Walking over to a cabinet by the door, he reached inside, then placed a silver key on the table. He didn't dare touch her again. "This is your key to the diner. Do *not* lose it, or I'll have to rekey the entire building."

She nodded, looking stoic. He knew he could trust her. And yet, he'd trusted her once with his heart, and look how that turned out.

"Why don't you lift the blinds on the windows and unlock the front door? I think we're ready to open for business," he said.

She took a quick inhale, as if she was facing a firing squad. Her cheeks flooded a pretty shade of pink, and her blue eyes flickered with a bit of doubt. Then it was gone and she stood, squared her shoulders with determination and walked to the doorway. As she paused in the threshold and turned, he thought he should say something encouraging. But he didn't get the chance.

"*Danke* again for giving me this job, Caleb. I really do appreciate it," she said.

Then she was gone. He watched from the cutout into the dining room as she went to the front door. A Closed sign hung in the window. She turned it to read Open, then fumbled with the key he'd given her. Finally, she unlocked the door, then stepped over to the work area to check the coffee maker and syrup decanters. He hated to admit it, but she seemed thoughtful and conscientious of things he hadn't even told her about.

As he chopped fresh vegetables for the salad bar, he thought perhaps he could assign this task to Tessa starting tomorrow. She caught on fast and was quicker than his mother. Of course, he would never tell his *mamm* that. She was older now, and it might hurt her feelings. But maybe Tessa really could make a difference for them. *Mamm* could still help out now and then, but they could slow the pace for her. She could take things a little easier.

The bell over the front door tinkled as two *Englisch* ranchers sauntered in and sat up at the front counter. Caleb recognized them immediately. Hank Wilkins and Chuck Goodspeed. They were regulars. Good ol' boys who came in for their morning coffee, a long chat and an occasional plate of pancakes, bacon and eggs.

Caleb braced himself to see what Tessa might do. If she floundered, he'd step in to help. But over time, he'd find it difficult to cook and train her at the same time.

To Caleb's surprise, she immediately filled two glasses with ice water and snatched up two menus as she headed toward the men. Having heard the bell, Doris came from the back office to help.

"You new here?" Hank asked as Tessa set a menu before each man.

"Yes, sir." She spoke respectfully in perfect English. Holding her notepad and pen aloft, she was ready to take their order.

"What's yer name?" Hank asked.

"Tessa, sir."

Without opening the menu, Chuck pushed it toward her. "I don't need this, Tessa. I know what I want. A short stack, two eggs, bacon and coffee. Black."

Tessa's pen moved full speed as Doris joined her, standing back to offer assistance if needed.

"How would you like your eggs, sir?" Tessa asked.

"Over easy," Chuck said.

"I'll have the same, except I need cream and sugar." Hank doffed his cowboy hat and set it on the counter.

Tessa inclined her head. "Coming right up."

Doris nodded her approval, then reached for two cups and filled them with coffee while Tessa snapped the order up. Caleb was looking right at her through the cutout, and their eyes locked for several moments. Then Tessa turned away and retrieved the cream and sugar dishes, placing them in front of Hank.

"*Gut* job," Doris whispered to Tessa as she passed by to serve the customers their coffee.

Yes, Caleb realized Tessa was doing fine so far, considering it was her first day on the job.

She didn't speak, but her countenance changed. And considering that the Amish didn't offer a lot of praise—mainly because it led to *Hochmut*, the pride of men—Tessa looked highly relieved. In fact, she almost beamed. And for some odd reason, Caleb couldn't help feeling proud of her simple accomplishment. He didn't know why. He didn't want her here. This was a mistake—he knew it deep in his bones. Yes, he hoped she would work hard. Her efforts would reflect well on the diner and be good for business. But his feelings were more than that. Something he didn't understand.

As he reached for a carton of eggs and cracked four of them over the grill, he couldn't forget what had happened earlier. Tessa's eye had been stung by ketchup. And knowing she was in pain, he'd acted without thinking, snatching up a clean dishrag and wringing it with water. He'd been cleansing her eye before he realized what he was doing. For a few scant moments in time, all that mattered was helping her. Making sure she was all right. And that scared him half to death. Because getting close to her again could have devastating results. For him and his broken heart.

He couldn't forget the way she'd kissed her little son's forehead earlier that morning while the boy was still asleep. He had no doubt she loved the child dearly. He'd overheard her comment about Sam being on a farm and felt compelled to have them come over to his place after work. It'd be good for the boy, but being near Tessa and Sam on a daily basis was going to be more than difficult. Because they were a constant reminder of the *familye* Caleb might never have, and he couldn't help resenting her for taking that away from him.

He must keep his distance. That was all there was to it. Tessa had hurt him deeply. Almost more than he could stand. He'd only just started to recover, and here she came, rushing back into his life. He couldn't take the chance she'd hurt him again. No, sirree. No closeness. Not even friendship. And that was that.

Chapter Four

They closed the restaurant promptly at seven that evening. They hadn't been busy, but Tessa had learned a lot. She locked the front door, turned out the lights in the dining room, then joined her son in the kitchen. He sat at a small table with Doris. The boy impatiently waited as Caleb served them each a bowl of leftover chicken soup and a plate of meat loaf, corn and mashed potatoes with gravy for supper. Resting on the sideboard was a dish of warm blueberry cobbler for each of them.

"*Gut*, you're here. *Komm* and sit." Doris beckoned to her.

Tessa slid into her seat, realizing they were waiting for her. This was the first time she'd been able to rest, and she breathed a low sigh of relief. Her feet ached, but she'd survived her first day and it hadn't been so bad.

As Caleb slid their bowls of soup onto the table, he joined them and bowed his head. It was the signal for a blessing on the food. Without question, they each joined him in a silent prayer. After a few moments, they ate. Only then did Tessa notice how hungry she was. Though she'd been feeding people all day, she'd hardly had time to eat much herself. Now, she was ravenous. And from the way Sam was gobbling down his meat loaf, he was hungry, too.

"*Ach*, slow down, *sohn*. You'll get a *bauchweh*," she cautioned with a laugh.

"*Ne*, my stomach feels fine. I want to hurry so we can go to Caleb's farm. He said I can help him milk the cows tonight," Sam said.

The boy sounded happy and excited. At her brother's farm, Sam was deemed too young to milk cows, though he'd always wanted to try. Tessa's brother couldn't be bothered teaching him, so the boy was relegated to dumping the garbage instead. Tessa was amazed Caleb had made the offer.

She glanced at the man, noticing how he ducked his head over his meal. He peered at Sam from over the top of his glass of milk.

"You'll like our farm," Doris said. "We have two baby calves and six little piglets. You can help your *mamm* and me feed them."

"Really? *Onkel* Wayne never lets me feed his pigs. He says I'll get trampled by the sow." Sam's eyes were wide and gleaming as he scooped mashed potatoes and gravy into his mouth.

"*Ach*, we have our pen set up so you can feed the piglets but the sow can't get underneath where the babies eat. Otherwise, she'd consume all their food and possibly hurt them, too. Besides, I'll stay with you. You'll be safe enough," Doris said.

"Okay!" Sam exclaimed, eating even faster, if that was possible.

A low sound came from the back of Caleb's throat, and Tessa glanced his way. Though he had his head bowed over his plate, she was fairly sure she heard a low chuckle rumbling in his chest.

"Slow down," Tessa told her son, using her mother's tone of voice. "You can't go before we're all finished eating and the dishes are washed. So, chew your food properly."

Sam frowned. "Ahh! Can't y'all hurry up?"

Tessa and Doris laughed, but Caleb turned away, burying a cough behind the back of his hand. Tessa was almost certain he was laughing, too. And that didn't make sense. After all, Sam was her son, and Caleb had no reason to like the boy, much less be amused by him.

Within minutes, they'd eaten their supper. Tessa washed the dishes while Doris dried and Caleb did some prep work for tomorrow morning's special of chicken-fried steak. And soon, they had locked the back door and stepped out into the alley, where Caleb's buggy awaited them. The horse lounged beside a watering trough. The summer day was still bright, the azure sky holding only a few fluffy white clouds. They had maybe another hour before the sun hid behind the western mountains…plenty of time to finish their farm chores.

As Caleb showed Tessa how to secure the back door, Doris maneuvered herself so that she was first inside the buggy. Caleb helped his mom and Sam as they sat in the back seat. Then, Caleb offered his arm to

Tessa. Knowing it would bring a rush of memories she was trying hard to forget, she hesitated, not wanting to touch him again. But there was no way around it without being rude.

Clasping his forearm, she hopped up as quickly as possible. They waited while Caleb calmly walked around to the driver's side and climbed in. Taking the lead lines in a practiced grip, he released the brake and slapped the leather lightly against the horse's back.

"*Komm* on, Tommy. Let's go *heemet*," he called.

As if sensing he was about to be fed in a cozy stall, the horse's head came up, and he stepped forward almost eagerly. The buggy lurched into motion as they headed down Main Street, the gelding moving at a fast trot.

Within minutes, they pulled off the main road and onto the long, dirt lane leading directly to Caleb's farm. The house stood off to one side, a dusty blue color with white trim and a wraparound porch. Several Adirondack chairs sat on the porch for relaxing in the evening. The structure was surrounded by meticulous green lawns, flower beds filled with yellow and orange marigolds, and baskets of hot pink petunias hanging from the canopy overhead.

Chickens squawked and scattered in the yard as they passed. On the other side of the graveled driveway, an enormous red barn, pigpens, corrals, sheds and a huge garden plot looked just as orderly. Fields of hay opened to Tessa's view. She wasn't surprised by what she saw. As a girl, she'd spent many hours at this farm. At one time, she'd thought she would one day live and raise her children here. It was obvious Caleb took as good care of the place as his father before him.

Upon seeing them, the milk cows started moving from the pasture toward the barn, knowing instinctively it was time to be milked and fed for the night. Two enormous draft horses did likewise, coming in for their nightly ration of hay and grain. Everything seemed so tranquil and restive. So orderly and calm.

So homey and wonderful.

Caleb pulled the buggy to a halt in front of the barn. Sam was bouncing with excitement as Doris waited for Caleb to come around and help her down. Then Caleb lifted the little boy and swung him around before setting him on his feet. Sam cried out with glee, then immediately raced over to the pigpen, standing on tiptoe so he could see over the fence.

"Wait right there, Sam. Don't go inside until one of us is with you," Caleb called.

The boy waited obediently. Since he was too short to see over the fence effectively, he peered through the slats, trying to get a look at the animals inside.

Doris laughed and glanced at Tessa. "You and I had better get over there fast, before that *kind* climbs right inside the pen with that mother sow."

Tessa smiled, letting Caleb help her down. He handed her a bucket of food scraps he had saved from the diner. On a farm like this, very little went to waste. Without asking, she knew the scraps were for the pigs.

She immediately stepped away. As Caleb led the horse and buggy into the barn so he could remove the harness, she forced herself not to look back. Instead, she made her way over to the pigs, trying to ignore the feeling of Caleb's strong hands pressed gently against her waist.

Sure enough, the mother sow had six little piglets snorting and milling around in the pen with her. Handing the bucket of scraps to her son, Tessa supported the heavy weight as she helped him dump the contents into the sow's food trough. Snorting with delight, the pig ducked her head down and ate.

"For Sam's sake, I think we had best start our chores here," Doris said.

The woman led Tessa into the barn. Doris showed her where the calf and piglet supplement was stored, as well as the chicken feed. Sam stuck with them as they went outside to feed the smaller animals, exclaiming with pleasure as the piglets squealed and claimed their dinner. Then, Caleb appeared in the barn doorway.

"Sam, *komm* inside with me. I'm going to milk the cows now," Caleb called.

Without so much as a look in his mother's direction, Sam ran off like a shot. Since Tessa knew what she was doing, Doris went inside the house to get ready for bed. Seeing the weary drooping of the older woman's shoulders, Tessa didn't mind. It had been a long day, and Doris needed rest.

Having fed the chickens, Tessa entered the barn to return the feed can to its hook on the wall. The lowing of contented cattle drew her attention, and she stepped over to one of the stalls. Caleb sat on a three-legged stool behind a milk cow, his head bent low as he milked the animal. Sam was crouched between the man's legs, reaching forward to help. They didn't notice she was there.

"Pull gently but firmly," Caleb said in a low, almost reverent tone.

"My hands are too small," Sam complained.

"Don't worry, they will grow."

The whoosh of milk hitting the metal bucket filled the air.

"Look! I'm doing it, Caleb," Sam exclaimed in an excited whisper.

"*Ja*, you are. That's *gut*. You're getting the hang of it. You see? It doesn't matter how small you are. And in time, you'll be a grown man," Caleb said.

"Like you?" Sam asked.

"*Ja*, like me."

Tessa blinked, her eyes burning with sudden tears. Seeing her fatherless son with this man in this setting was almost more than she could stand. Though he'd tried, her older brother hadn't been this patient with Sam. After all, Wayne had a passel of kids of his own to raise. Sam was only four, and Wayne had older sons he needed to teach. He didn't really have the inclination to foster Tessa's boy. And Sam was hungry for the attention of a father figure in his life. Someone to spend a little time with him. Someone to look up to.

Someone like Caleb Yoder.

Tessa backed away before they saw her there and hurried out to the chicken coop to gather the evening eggs. As she worked, her heart was filled with regrets. If only she could go back in time, she would never have gone to Denver without Caleb by her side. In fact, she never wanted to leave his farm. But it was too late for them. She couldn't change things. She had to keep going forward.

As quietly as possible, so she wouldn't disturb Doris, she carried the basket of eggs into the house and cleaned them before stowing them inside the fridge. Then she returned to the barnyard. She was grateful her son seemed happy here. She was glad to be working on a farm again, too. It felt peaceful and wholesome to be among the livestock. Years ago, when she'd gone to Denver, she'd resented her way of life. It was too structured and too confining. But when she'd taken her job at the restaurant, she hadn't realized how much she might miss working on a farm. It was the Amish way of life, and she loved it now. Though she was tired from working a full day at the restaurant, this felt normal and familiar. She was glad to be here.

Looking up, she saw Caleb carrying two buckets of frothy white milk toward the house. Sam was right beside him, running to keep up with the man's long stride, talking animatedly.

"Do you think I can help you milk the cows again tomorrow?" Sam asked.

"*Ja*, of course," came the man's deep reply.

"Great! It was awesome!" Sam exclaimed.

Awesome? Where had her son learned such a word? Probably from the other children at church. It sounded so *Englisch*, and Tessa wasn't sure she liked it.

The two disappeared into the well house. She knew Caleb would store the milk there in that chilled environment until he was ready to use it at the diner.

A feeling of appreciation filled her heart. Even if Caleb didn't like her anymore, she was grateful for his tolerance and kindness toward her son. Sam was innocent and deserved a happy childhood. It was difficult raising a boy without a father. Considering her circumstances, Tessa had done the best she could. And once more, a feeling of regret threatened to overshadow the success of her long day. Suddenly, she was very tired. The sleepless night before and the long hours of work finally caught up with her. All she wanted was to go home, put Sam to bed and be alone with her thoughts.

Within an hour, the chores were finished. Standing in the yard, watching the sun fade behind the snow-capped mountains, Caleb stared at the barn. Surely there was something they'd missed. Some chores that remained undone. But no. They were all completed, and his mom had already gone to bed. He realized again what a fast, efficient worker Tessa was. More and more, he was seeing the advantage of hiring her to work for him.

Now, it was time to take her and Sam home to their little apartment over the diner. But as he went to hook Tommy up to the buggy again, he couldn't help feeling a bit resentful. Tessa and her boy belonged on a farm. They belonged here. With him. And if she hadn't run off to Denver all those years earlier and gotten herself caught with another man's child, this was exactly where they'd be living now.

Sam would have been his child. But that wasn't the case. Sam wasn't his son. Even so, Caleb couldn't be angry at the boy. He was completely innocent. In fact, Caleb liked having the kid follow him around, asking him a barrage of questions, getting in his way every time he turned around. Sam was guileless, kindhearted and eager to learn the ways of a farm. And it wasn't

Sam that Caleb begrudged. It was Tessa. But Caleb knew even that wasn't right. The Lord had taught patience, kindness and forgiveness. The tenets of Caleb's faith dictated that he should let go of his anger and forgive her. But no matter how hard he tried, he couldn't seem to overcome his harsh feelings toward her.

"Caleb?"

He whirled around, finding Tessa standing right behind him with Sam. She was holding the little boy's hand as he stifled a wide yawn. Sam was smiling, but looked sleepy. His batteries had finally wound down. And all Caleb could think was that he could neither shun these two nor accept them. So where did that leave them? Nowhere! He was Tessa's employer, nothing more.

The evening sunset painted a glow of pink and orange behind them. Though Tessa stood proud and tall, she looked overly tired, too. He knew she'd worked hard that day, but she hadn't complained once. That wasn't surprising. The Amish work ethic was second to none. No doubt the town fund-raiser would go much easier next week because of her. And though it was on the tip of Caleb's tongue to praise her and ask how she was doing, he bit the words back. Praise wasn't something the Amish did very often, but maybe Tessa could use a kind word right now.

"You have done well today" was all he could manage.

It was enough. She smiled, so bright that he thought he'd never seen anything so beautiful in all his life.

"*Danke* for being so kind to Sam," she said.

He nodded, not daring to respond. Because then he

might tell her what he really thought, and she'd be offended and run for the hills. But it was fun to be with Sam. The child was so excited to learn everything. Though the kid got in his way and spilled the grain, Caleb didn't have the heart to scold him or push him away.

"I've cleaned and put the eggs away in your fridge inside the house," Tessa said. "If you don't have anything else for me to do, Sam and I are ready to go *heemet*, when you're ready to take us."

He indicated the buggy. "We can leave now."

He waited for her and Sam to proceed him. She reached to lift Sam up inside, but Caleb didn't make a move to help her. As she struggled with the weight of her son, he instantly regretted being rude. Feeling guilty, he offered his arm to her as she climbed inside with her boy.

During the short ride to the diner, Sam sat between them. The day had caught up with the child, and he slumped against Caleb. When the boy burrowed closer, a hot flush filled Caleb's face with heat. His heart gave a powerful squeeze, and he couldn't help feeling protective of this little boy and his mother.

"I'm sorry." Tessa reached over and pulled Sam against her.

Caleb didn't stop her. His emotions waged a war inside his heart and mind. Anger warred with compassion. He felt both frozen and hot all at the same time.

She draped an arm around the child's shoulders and pulled him in close against her, smoothing Sam's hair with her hand. By the time they arrived, the boy was fast asleep.

Caleb parked the buggy next to the outside stairs leading up to Tessa's apartment and climbed out.

"I'll get the *bu*," he told her.

Hurrying around, he helped her down, then reached inside to pull Sam into his arms. The boy didn't awaken as Caleb carried him up the narrow stairs with Tessa following behind. She quickly unlocked the door. Caleb stood cradling Sam in the small living area and waited while she turned on a gas-powered light. Thick shadows gathered around the sparse furnishings of the apartment, and he noticed everything was tidy and in order.

"Bring him here," Tessa whispered as she beckoned to him.

He followed her down the hallway to Sam's room and laid the child on his narrow bed. As he stood back, Tessa quickly removed Sam's socks and shoes. The summer evening was still warm, but she tucked a blanket around him. Caleb watched her motherly movements in silence, allowing himself to ponder what it would have been like if they had married and this was their son. They might have had other children, too. For just a moment, he could almost pretend Sam and Tessa were his and this was a natural, everyday occurrence…putting their child to bed after a busy day of work. But it wasn't reality, and Caleb did himself a disservice by thinking otherwise.

In silence, they stepped out of the room, and Tessa pulled the door so it was slightly ajar. She could easily hear Sam if the boy cried out.

"He's really worn-out. *Danke* for being so kind to

him," she whispered as she accompanied Caleb back to the kitchen area.

"You're *willkomm*," he returned.

They stood there in silence for several moments. Caleb didn't know what to say. It felt as if his heart was pounding in his ears. Once again, his mind was filled with questions he longed to ask her. Explanations he hoped might clarify what had happened so long ago and give him a transparent way to forgive her for what she'd done. But no answers were forthcoming, and he wouldn't ask. Not again.

Those old feelings of sadness, disappointment and fury gripped his heart.

"*Ach*, I best get going. I'll see you in the morning," he said.

"*Ja*, in the morning," she whispered back.

He walked to the door, turned the knob and stepped out onto the landing. From his peripheral vision, he saw her pale face as she gave a little wave, then shut the portal behind him. He waited to hear the click of the dead bolt before he left. And as he walked down the stairs, climbed into his buggy and drove home, he'd never felt more alone in all his life.

Chapter Five

❧

"Where do you want me to put the warming ovens?"

Tessa paused in her chore of spreading white plastic coverings over the tables they'd set up for customers to eat at. Standing beneath a large canopy in the city park, she glanced over her shoulder. It was the day of the town fund-raiser. Since Caleb was busy assembling his gas-powered barbecue, she found herself in the unique position of directing much of the work.

"Let's put them over here." She jutted her chin toward the farthest serving table. She'd been using masking tape to hold the table coverings down so they wouldn't blow away with the light summer breeze. Tossing the roll into her basket of supplies, she immediately ran to help carry the heavy load.

Caleb had hired two women from their congregation to assist with the one-day event. While he provided the heavy muscle to assemble the canopy and carry most of the hefty equipment, Naomi Fisher was now packing one of the ovens by herself.

Working together, they set the silver warming oven

down and Naomi plugged it into a gas-powered generator Caleb had set up for them so they could receive power.

"There! That should work efficiently enough." Naomi nodded with satisfaction and dusted off her hands in finality.

Tessa smiled at the woman. Naomi always saw the practical side of things. A stocky, matronly woman with a cheery smile, she was just as old as Doris, yet she was still strong and capable of hard work.

Though it was barely ten o'clock in the morning, the summer day was already quite warm. Birds twittered overhead in the treetops, the sky an azure blue. But Tessa didn't have time to admire those things for long. She rolled the long sleeves of her dress up above her elbows and took a deep inhale of fragrant air. The fund-raiser wouldn't officially open for another hour, but the park was already filled with *Englisch* people who were setting up their own booths. Popcorn, cotton candy, snow cones and pulled taffy, as well as a variety of crafts and artwork were on display. All the proceeds would go toward the new swimming pool.

Hannah Schwartz, the other woman Caleb had hired, stood nearby, unfolding metal chairs to set in front of the eating tables. "Do you think we'll have a big turnout today?"

"*Ja*, the whole town will be here, and all our people, too," Naomi said.

Tessa nodded, knowing the Amish would flock to this event. A quilt auction was scheduled for two o'clock, and her people had donated four beautiful queen-size quilts. All the women in Tessa's *Gmay* had been working on them every chance they got for six solid months. In the end, it had become a feverish chore to finish them on time. In a teeny town like this, they didn't have many special events. It was a real treat for everyone, *Englisch* and Amish alike.

"I think you're right. We'll have a *gut* turnout. The town will be able to buy their swimming pool soon enough," Caleb said.

He had unloaded and set up his gas-powered barbecue nearby. Just now, he was digging through a box and pulling out wide serving trays and the long-handled spatulas and tongs he would need to flip burgers, hot dogs and chicken breasts. Bottles of barbecue sauce sat waiting on another small table nearby.

"How do you want this set up?" Naomi asked him, gesturing to the serving tables.

He glanced at Tessa, then turned away. "Whatever Tessa wants. She's in charge of that."

Her mouth dropped open in surprise. His deferential treatment touched her heart, and yet he barely looked at her. After almost a week of working daily at the diner, Tessa had become a pro at waiting on tables. More and more, Caleb was giving her the freedom to do as she liked. As long as things ran smoothly and the customers were pleased, Caleb seemed happy. But Tessa sensed a palpable friction between them and thought he was purposefully trying to avoid her at all costs. Not an easy thing to do, considering they were together all the time.

Tessa took a deep inhale. "Let's put the hot foods at this end, away from Doris."

Doris currently sat on the other end of the long serving table with the cash box. The task of taking money was perfect for her since it would keep her off her feet while Tessa and the other women served the food. A big easel sign had been set up in the grass next to her to display the menu and food prices. Caleb had contributed the meat for the fundraiser. And considering the Amish would never use the swimming pool, Tessa thought that was quite generous of him.

"We can set the hamburger and hot dog buns nearby. That way, customers can pay Doris first, then they'll move along the assembly line as we serve them their fruit salad, beans and potatoes and give them a bag of chips and a bun before they move over to Caleb's grill for their meat. He can plop their hamburger or hot dog right on their bun. Then, they can move over to the condiment table and sit down to enjoy their meal."

As she spoke, she pointed to each position and made other assignments so everyone knew what was expected of them.

"That's a *gut* plan. It'll work great," Doris said.

"We can put the condiments on this smaller table over here, and people can help themselves with that." Naomi pointed to a shady spot nearby, beneath the span of a tall elm tree.

"That's perfect. Let's do it," Tessa said.

They all went back to work. Naomi immediately placed the canisters of ketchup, mustard, pickle relish and onions on the table. Tessa didn't have to tell the women twice. They were fully mature, experienced workers with numerous children of their own. They'd been preparing at the diner for two days now and had gotten up extra early that morning to slice fresh fruits and vegetables and cook the baked beans and cheesy potatoes.

Their group was happy in their labors, chatting in *Deitsch*. Tessa felt good to be among friends. Lovina Lapp, another member of their congregation, had offered to watch Sam while Tessa was busy in the park. Caleb had dropped Sam off at the Lapp farm earlier. Lovina was their midwife and newly married to Jonah Lapp. She was also expecting her first child. Tessa was content, knowing her son was safe and happy so she could focus on her work.

Thinking about Caleb, Tessa glanced over to where he was setting up a generator to run their cooler chests. They didn't want anyone to get food poisoning and had prepared accordingly. Even though they didn't use electricity in their homes, the Amish were still held accountable by the health inspectors.

Caleb was turned away from her, his head bowed over a piece of equipment as he knelt on one knee in the grass. The corded muscles across his back rippled as he moved a heavy generator, then used a screwdriver to tighten down a screw. Tessa tried not to stare. She really did. But…

"Well, howdy, little lady."

Tessa jerked around, startled out of her wits. A tall *Englisch* man stood on the opposite side of the table from her. Dressed in blue jeans, scuffed cowboy boots and a red checked shirt, he also wore a scruffy cowboy hat and two days' worth of stubble on his chin. She immediately caught the strong scent of alcohol on his breath, and her nose twitched with repugnance as she stepped back and lifted a hand to her face. Thankfully, the table stood as a barrier between them.

"Um, hello," she said, feeling a bit embarrassed as she recovered her composure. "Can I help you?"

He leaned across the table, resting his elbows on the top as he smiled wide. He was missing one tooth in the front.

"Sure, you can help me. My name's Bryce. Bryce Jackson. What's your name, pretty girl?" he asked.

His speech was languid and slightly slurred, and she thought maybe he was drunk. She'd heard about men who consumed too much alcohol but never really met one…until that night in Denver when she'd gone to an *Englisch* house party. There'd been numerous young men at that event, all of them dancing and drinking and laughing boisterously. At the time, Tessa had been intrigued and eager to join in the fun. She'd been so naive and gullible. Then, her *Englisch* girlfriend introduced her to a handsome young man who was twenty-five years old and seemed so mature, composed and interesting. He'd been dressed well and spoke courteously, and she'd been impressed. He'd gotten her a drink, and they'd sat in a corner of the living room and talked for a while. He'd been so polite and kind, and she'd felt happy and safe. Then her memories became fuzzy and she couldn't remember much after that. Now, she realized how foolish she'd been to ever trust a stranger.

"What can I do for you?" she asked, purposefully neglecting to give him her name. The Amish kept themselves aloof around the *Englisch*—with good reason. The *Englisch* were people of the world. Tessa had learned that lesson harder than most Amish girls she knew.

"You know, you're awful purty, for an Amish girl. Most of your women look quite plain. But you're downright beautiful. If you take that cap off your head... how long is your hair, anyway?"

He rudely snatched at her prayer *kapp*, and she dodged to the side, lifting her hands to shield herself.

"Please don't touch me, sir," she said.

"Sir?" He laughed exuberantly. "I'm not a sir. I'm just Bryce." His eyes narrowed, but his crude smile didn't fade. "What are you serving here, anyway?"

He glanced at the tables and food, which hadn't been uncovered and set out, yet. Tessa was conscious of Naomi and Hannah moving toward her. Doris stood up from her chair, one hand still resting on the cash box, which was filled with change. All the women frowned with disapproval at Bryce. But where was Caleb? Tessa couldn't see him.

"Our menu is posted over there, if you'd like to take a look." Tessa pointed toward the easel. "But I'm afraid we're not open yet. If you'd like to come back in an hour or so, we'll be ready to serve you then."

She tried to smile but gasped when Bryce rounded the table and came toward her in the serving area, which was meant for employees only. She backed up, but he moved so fast, she didn't have time to get away. Naomi and Hannah hurried over to her. But what could they do? The Amish were pacifists. They wouldn't fight back, no matter what.

"I'm not interested in a hamburger. I'd rather talk to you," Bryce said.

He wrapped an arm around her waist and pulled her in close. She lifted her arms up to try and put some distance between them, but didn't push or use force at all. A blaze of panic zipped through her like a bolt of lightning. Dark, woozy memories flooded her, of being handled roughly by cruel, painful hands. Filled with terror, she turned her face aside when Bryce leaned in close. She tried to get free, but he held her tight. His foul breath made her stomach churn, and she was forced to duck her head to keep him from planting a kiss on her face.

"Please let me go!" she cried.

"Hey, sweetheart, there's no need to be like that. I won't hurt you. What time do you get off work?" he asked.

She didn't get the chance to respond. Caleb came up behind the man and tapped on Bryce's shoulder.

"Excuse me, sir," Caleb said.

Bryce turned and staggered, leaning heavily against Tessa. She would have fallen flat beneath his weight, but Caleb latched on to Bryce's arm and held him upright. Naomi and Hannah immediately pulled Tessa into the protection of their arms.

"Whoa, I feel dizzy," Bryce exclaimed, lifting a hand to his head. His hat dropped to the ground, revealing his greasy, matted hair that looked like it hadn't been washed or combed in several days.

Holding the cash box with one arm, Doris quickly joined them, reaching to cup Tessa's face as she peered into her eyes.

"Are you *allrecht*?" she asked quietly in *Deitsch*.

Tessa met the woman's eyes, breathing heavily, her

heart racing. She tried to calm herself, but realized she was trembling like a leaf. That was when she realized they'd drawn a small crowd of people. *Englischers* were staring at them, assessing the situation and scowling at Bryce.

"*Ja*, I'm okay," Tessa whispered to Doris.

"Can you stand on your own, sir?" Caleb asked Bryce.

Caleb was doing an admirable job of being polite, but Tessa saw his expression. He was smiling, but his eyes were sharp as flint. He strategically placed himself between Bryce and the women, and Tessa had never been so glad to see him in all her life.

"Let go! I can stand by myself," Bryce growled as he jerked away.

Caleb backed away, resting his hands at his sides as he spoke politely. "I'm sorry, sir, but you can't be on this side of the table. It's a violation of the health code. This is our service area, and only my employees can be back here."

Bryce looked at Tessa, and she flinched inwardly.

"I just wanna talk to the purty girl. Get outta my way," he said, trying to brush Caleb aside.

Caleb didn't budge. He didn't raise his hands or fight back in any way, but he braced his feet beneath him and planted himself in the middle of the *Englisch* man's path.

"I'm sorry, sir, but she's working. I need to ask you to leave now," Caleb said.

"Why, you…" Bryce doubled up his fist and took a shot at the Amish man.

Caleb simply dodged the punch. Bryce was too

drunk to react, and his body slammed against one of the tables. Paper plates, utensils and serving platters rattled, with some of the packages of utensils dropping to the ground. Bryce regained his balance and threw an ugly glare at Caleb.

Anyone else might think Caleb was being kind and quiet and calm. But Tessa knew better when she saw his fists and biceps tighten. With his back turned toward her, she couldn't see his face. He was shielding her, protecting her, the only way he could. But would he strike Bryce? His body language told her that he was furious. How far could Bryce push him before Caleb lost his temper? He must not use force. He could be shunned by their people for doing such a thing. She hated that she was causing Caleb any difficulty. And in that moment, she wished she was anywhere but here.

Caleb stared at Bryce, wishing the man would figure out that he wasn't going to get to Tessa again and go away.

Clenching his hands, Caleb watched the other man carefully, prepared to dodge another punch if necessary. He was a pacifist, but he had a right to avoid being hurt, if possible.

When he'd seen Bryce manhandling Tessa, something had hardened inside him. Something mean and ugly. A rage he'd never felt before had boiled up inside his chest. The emotion had zipped through him so fast, he didn't understand where it came from. He wanted to pound Bryce to a pulp—a feeling that was completely alien to him. He knew it wasn't right. The tenets of his faith dictated that he should love everyone as himself, including a drunken ne'er-do-well like Bryce Jackson.

Jesus had taught that they should love all *Gott*'s children. But even if it meant he might be shunned by his Amish people forevermore, Caleb was not about to let Bryce touch Tessa ever again. Not if he could do something to stop it. And that didn't make sense. Because Caleb didn't love her now. She was a child of *Gott*, but she wasn't Caleb's concern. Not anymore. He was her boss and that was all. Wasn't it?

Forcing himself to relax his hands, Caleb stood his ground and waited. He knew Bryce well. He was one of the regulars that came into the diner all the time. At the age of thirty, Bryce's drinking had caused a dishevelment of appearance and a harshness to come into his face that made him look closer to fifty.

Though he was rather brash, loud and rowdy, Bryce was usually peaceful enough. But he was always unkempt and smelled of alcohol. Caleb had overheard customers in the diner say that Bryce's wife had taken his son and left him a year earlier, after he'd lost his job. Now, Bryce was a full alcoholic and couldn't seem to get his life back together. Occasionally, the man didn't even have enough money to pay his food bill at the restaurant. Though he didn't approve of the man's life, Caleb had gotten into a habit of overlooking the shortage. Caleb figured if he could get a decent, hot meal into Bryce, it might help the man stave off the booze and rebuild his life.

"Hey, Bryce! What are you doing, buddy?"

Caleb looked to where a crowd of *Englisch* people had gathered around his food booth. Hank Wilkins, one of his other regulars, stepped forward and took Bryce by the arm.

"Look what you did, man," Hank said, pointing to where Hannah was picking up the plastic utensils that had fallen to the ground.

Thankfully, the utensils were still wrapped in their original packaging and not contaminated. They wouldn't need to be thrown away. With everything else he had to do that day, Caleb didn't need the chore of running over to the grocery store to buy more. Besides the fact that the store was probably closed today.

Chuck Goodspeed joined Hank and took Bryce's other arm. Between the two men, they successfully pulled Bryce a safe distance away from the booth.

"I wanna talk to the purty Amish girl," Bryce cried, turning to look over his shoulder as he endeavored to pull free of the men's solid grips.

"I know, but Tessa is working right now. She can't visit with you," Chuck said.

"Tessa? Is that her name? That's purty, just like her," Bryce said.

"Yeah, and you don't want her to get fired, do you?" Chuck asked.

"No! No, she can't get fired," Bryce said, no longer fighting the two men.

"You can't go behind the tables. That's for the service people only. Do you wanna get them in trouble with the health inspector?" Chuck asked.

"No, I don't wanna get Tessa in no trouble," Bryce said, seeming almost humble and childlike now.

The man blinked tiredly and stumbled. Chuck and

Hank caught him, practically carrying Bryce as the inebriated man's legs buckled beneath him.

"Come on. We'll take you home where you can sleep it off," Hank said.

"But I don't wanna go home. I wanna talk to Tessa some more," Bryce said as they tried to shuffle him toward the parking lot.

The crowd of people stared after them, snapping pictures on their cell phones, mumbling together about what was going on.

"Not right now. She's working, remember?" Chuck hurried the man toward a pickup truck where he opened the passenger door, and the two men heaved Bryce inside.

While Chuck went around to the driver's seat, Hank slid in next to Bryce so they sandwiched the man between them on the seat. Watching all of this, Caleb breathed a sigh of relief, knowing Bryce couldn't escape them now. The drama was finally over with.

The crowd of people slowly dispersed, laughing and talking among themselves about what had happened. Caleb knew it would be all over town by noon and give the townsfolk lots of fodder to discuss as they wandered around the venue and attended the afternoon auction.

Turning, Caleb sought out Tessa. He didn't want her to be the topic of gossip. The Amish purposefully kept to themselves. They tried to go unnoticed. But that couldn't be helped today.

Tessa stood with his mother and the two other Amish women, her eyes wide, her face drained of color. She looked badly shaken, and he felt the urge to comfort her somehow. But what could he say?

"Tessa, are you *allrecht*?" he asked, feeling angry at her for some reason and not knowing why. After all, this hadn't been her fault. From what he'd witnessed, she was completely innocent.

She nodded, her voice a thin whisper. "I... I'm fine."

But she wasn't fine. He could see that in her stunned, wan expression. Though she'd done her best to offset the situation, she was badly shaken.

"Do you need to sit down for a while?" he asked, forcing himself not to enfold her in his arms and comfort her. He couldn't do that, no matter how much concern he felt for her right now. Instead, he forced himself to squelch his compassion. He was so confused right now, his feelings waffling back and forth. Never again could he trust this woman. His heart couldn't take it. But neither could he stand to see her hurt by a brute like Bryce.

"*Ne*, I... I'll be fine. I... I'd like to get back to work now and forget it ever happened, please." She stepped away from the women and reached for a napkin dispenser. As she filled it with paper napkins, her hands visibly trembled.

Caleb watched her for several moments, wondering why she was so upset. Yes, the scene with Bryce had been disturbing for all of them, but Tessa seemed overly shocked and dismayed. She seemed almost...

Terrified.

He glanced at his mother and whispered low for her ears alone. "*Mamm*, let's keep an eye on her. I think she'll be okay, but I don't want her to faint or something. If Bryce returns, you come get me immediately."

Doris nodded. "*Ja*, we'll take *gut* care of her, *sohn*. Don't you worry."

But that was just it. He was worried about Tessa and he didn't understand why. He was afraid he was missing something here. Something big. Because Tessa's reaction to Bryce wasn't normal. She'd been more than afraid. She'd been panicked and desperate to get away from the man. And other than the obvious reasons, Caleb wasn't sure why.

He went back to work, hurrying so he had all the generators set up and the refrigerator system working before they opened for business in another fifteen minutes. He'd better get some hamburgers on the grill right now. It would be a long day. But even though this was a fund-raiser, it was a good draw for the diner's business.

He slapped several hamburger patties and hot dogs on the grill, then added a few marinated chicken breasts. The sizzling smoke and tantalizing aroma of barbecue filled the air. He salted the patties and picked up his long-handled spatula, unable to get the vision of Tessa's wide, tearful eyes out of his mind. What was this hold she still had over him? He didn't love her anymore. They weren't even a couple now. And they never would be again. It would be better to put some distance between them. But how? They worked closely together every day of the week.

Well, he'd have to try. He could talk business with her and nothing more. No extra chitchat or asking about Sam or her family. Nothing that didn't have to do with the diner or her chores on his farm. She'd broken his heart once before, and he couldn't take the chance of getting close to her again. Not as long as he had breath in his body.

Chapter Six

Sunday morning, Tessa awoke at her usual time but languished in bed another twenty minutes. The diner was closed for the Sabbath and she didn't have any farm chores, so she enjoyed the quiet respite. They did have church at the Burkholders' farm that morning, but it wasn't far. She and Sam should be able to walk the distance within thirty minutes.

Heaving a deep sigh, she sat up and flung the blankets back as she swung her legs over the side of the bed. The fund-raiser yesterday had been tiring, to say the least. The hard work was to be expected, but her encounter with Bryce Jackson had shaken her more than she realized. Once Hank and Chuck had escorted Bryce away from Caleb's food booth, she'd been more than relieved. But it had taken her an hour to stop shaking. Though she didn't understand why, the encounter had brought her past rushing back in a haze of fear and panic.

It was completely unexpected. One moment, she'd been fine. The next moment, she'd wanted to hit and scream at Bryce to leave her alone. Even now, she felt a bit disconcerted by the event. Like she could do nothing to stop what was happening to her. And she didn't like feeling that way at all. Though she was a pacifist, it hadn't been easy for her to remain calm and unaffected. Only her faith in *Gott* had gotten her through. She'd felt bullied and out of control, and she didn't like that.

And then Caleb had stepped in. Shielding her from Bryce. Protecting her without a bit of force.

As the day had worn on, she'd tried to pretend she was unfazed, but her hands had trembled, and she'd dropped an entire container of cheesy potatoes. Caleb hadn't said a word as he'd helped her pick it up. Doris had rushed to her side, hugging her tight to show her support. Thankfully, the long pan had landed flat on the grass without spilling its contents, and they were able to salvage it. Caleb had glanced at her, a thoughtful frown creasing his forehead, his eyes filled with concern. Now, the scene was over with, and she could put it behind her. But something had strengthened inside her since then. The determination to never allow any man to make her feel frightened and out of control again. Not Bryce Jackson. Not anyone.

Reaching for her bathrobe, she pulled it on and padded across the floor in bare feet. Peeking into Sam's room, she found him still sleeping. The first glimmers of early-morning sun streamed through the open window, bathing his room in faint light. His eyes were closed in slumber, his long lashes lying against his cheeks. His lips were slightly parted as he breathed evenly. A thatch of golden hair had fallen across his brow. He looked so peaceful. So sweet and innocent.

Careful not to disturb him, Tessa sat on the edge of his mattress and gazed at his endearing face. Though it was still early, she knew they would quickly run out of time if she didn't awaken him soon. They both needed baths and breakfast. But she lingered for just a couple more minutes, drinking him in. Marveling at how *Gott* had created such a perfect and amazing little boy. She could watch him for hours and never get enough. Though she'd gone through something horrible years earlier, the Lord had blessed her with this incredible child. She felt humbled that *Gott* would trust her to raise this little boy to be a man.

If only she hadn't lost Caleb in the process.

"Sam." She said his name softly as she reached out and caressed his cheek, awakening him slowly.

He blinked his eyes open. Brown eyes that didn't look like hers. She couldn't help wondering about her child's father. She could barely remember his handsome face now, but she knew Sam had his eyes and nose.

The boy gazed at her for several moments. Then a languid smile spread across his face.

"Mammi."

He said her name with affection, and her heart gave a powerful squeeze. How she adored this child.

"You're going to have to get up and get dressed if we're to arrive at church on time," she said, a feeling of unconditional love swelling inside her chest.

Sam sat up fast and flung the covers back. *"Ja*, I get to see Benuel and Elijah today."

With the incentive of seeing his friends firmly in mind, he scrambled off the bed and hurried into the bathroom across the hall. Tessa followed, wetting a clean washcloth under the faucet.

"Wait till I see Elijah. I've got so much to tell him. They're not gonna believe all that's happened to me," Sam said.

Tessa smiled as she wrung out the cloth and washed the sleep from his face, then combed his hair. "You really are excited to see your friends, aren't you?"

"*Ja!* I haven't seen them in forever!"

She chuckled. It had been two long weeks since the boys had been together. Tessa figured that must seem like forever to a young child. She wished she could take her son on more playdates, but it wasn't possible with her current work schedule. Thankfully, Doris took Sam to the park every day. But it was rather solitary for an Amish child. Sam should have lots of siblings. He deserved a normal *familye* life with a mom and dad. And Tessa couldn't give that to him.

"Benuel won't believe how hard I've worked at the diner and on Caleb's farm," Sam continued, breathing a heavy sigh.

"*Ja*, you're a *gut* worker. But remember not to grumble about it. That's most unbecoming to the Lord."

She didn't mind praising her son, but wanted him to be humble about his labors. It was important to teach her son the benefits of work, so she had started letting him help her fill the condiment and salt and pepper containers and wrap eating utensils in napkins. Sam had a willing attitude, but she wanted him to be modest about it, too.

"You shouldn't brag about your chores nor complain. It's expected by *Gott* that we work hard, but it's not something to flaunt or whine about. You don't want to draw attention to yourself because of your efforts," she said.

He tilted his head to one side. "Why not?"

"Because it's too prideful, and *Gott* wants us to be kind and humble."

Sam glanced at her, then looked down at his hands. "*Ne*, I don't want to be prideful. I'll try to be humble, *Mammi*."

Oh, her dear, sweet boy. He was so slow to anger or take offense, yet quick to repent and forgive others. How blessed she was to be this child's mother. She figured she learned more from him than he ever did from her.

Smiling to soften her words, she patted his cheek. "I know you will. Now, *komm* on. Let's both get dressed and I'll meet you in the kitchen for some breakfast."

"*Ja!*" He brightened right up, scurrying back to his room.

She made him a nice breakfast of scrapple and eggs, then they set out to walk to the Burkholders' farm. As predicted, they were running late, and she decided to cut across Caleb's field to make up some time. She carried a small basket with a cloth covering. It contained a Schnitz apple pie, her contribution for the lunch they would share with everyone after church services. As they walked through the tall grass, she held Sam's hand, enjoying the fragrant air and the warm, sunny day.

"*Mammi*," he said.

"*Ja?*"

"Do I have a *daed*?"

She stumbled but caught herself in time. Her mind scrambled as she thought what to say. Sam was only four years old. She'd known eventually he might ask this question. But not now. Not so soon. She thought she had more time to think about an appropriate response.

"Um, why do you ask?" she said, telling herself to keep walking, stalling for time.

"*Ach*, Elijah and Benuel both have *daeds*, but I don't. Why not?"

Tessa hopped over an irrigation ditch, then reached back to help Sam. She considered her words carefully. Finally, she answered as truthfully as possible.

"Their *vadders* are still in their lives, but your *daed* isn't," she said.

He glanced at her, looking bewildered. "Why not?"

"Because…because he didn't want to be with me," she said.

It was the truth. His name was Glen. For the life of her, she couldn't remember if he'd told her his last name or if she'd blocked it out. At the time, he'd told her he was from Denver. A college student attending the University of Colorado, majoring in foreign studies. He liked old movies, spoke Spanish and drank fruit-and-kale smoothies every morning for breakfast. That was all she knew about him, really. He'd drugged her, then taken advantage when she couldn't even defend herself. Obviously he didn't want to be with her. He'd just wanted to use her, then cast her aside like a used candy wrapper. And she figured her son was too young to understand all of that. Maybe one day, she would tell Sam everything. But not right now. Not on her life.

"I can't imagine him not wanting to be with you. You're the best *mudder* in the whole wide world."

She smiled, appreciating his kind words.

"I wish my *daed* was here now. Then maybe you wouldn't have to work so hard," Sam said.

Her son's thoughtfulness touched her deeply. She smiled, her heart filled with empathy. After all, it was perfectly logical for Sam to wonder about his father.

"I know, *liebchen*. But we will always have each other," she said.

"I wish Caleb was my *daed*. Then we could be a real *familye*," he said.

Her heart gave a heavy thud. "I... I know. He's a nice man, isn't he?"

"Yep, he's the best. He lets me help him in the kitchen and everything," Sam said.

They walked on in silence, and Tessa found herself lost in the past. At the time, Tessa had wanted some excitement in her life. That was why she'd insisted on going to Denver while she had the chance...with or without Caleb. Glen had seemed so dynamic and athletic. He was *Englisch* and so knowledgeable. So... worldly. All she'd ever known were Amish farmers and the smells of hay, livestock and manure. Glen was everything Caleb was not. Well-dressed. Educated. Intellectual.

Exotic.

Over the past five years, Tessa had come to appreciate the simple, steady reliability of a man like Caleb. He wasn't sophisticated or worldly, but he was honest and kind. Though they would never marry, she knew he would never hurt her the way Glen had done. Caleb would never use her, then disappear into the night. She'd taken Caleb for granted and lost him because she was too silly, impatient and foolish. She could never change the past, and that was what hurt most of all.

"Look, *Mammi*. A well."

Sam pointed to a dilapidated rock well that sat near the remains of a foundation where an old farmhouse used to be located. Grateful for the distraction, Tessa breathed a sigh of relief.

"*Ja*, Caleb's grandparents used to live here years ago," she said.

"Where did they go?"

"They died, sweetums."

"Oh. I wish Caleb could be my *daed*," Sam said.

Tessa gazed at her son, wishing he wouldn't say that.

Sam didn't notice. He was focused on the well. A bucket and pulley system of rotting wood was affixed to the crumbling rock surround. A board lay across the opening, as if that would deter animals and curious children from climbing inside. Before she could stop him, Sam ran to the well and peered over the edge.

"Sam!" she cried, hurrying after him.

She had just latched on to his arm and pulled him back when the board and some of the rocks gave way beneath his weight and fell into the dark hole below. In the process, she almost dropped her basket. A sickening thud told her the well had dried up. Otherwise, she figured she would have heard a splash. Looking down into the channel, she saw that it was lined with collapsing wood and stones. From the looks of things, there had already been cave-ins. Some of the timbers were rotting out and barely hanging in place. The entire well had become compromised by years of neglect. It was a dangerous hazard, that was for sure.

Pulling her son into her arms, Tessa hugged him tight. "Are you *allrecht*?"

He nodded solemnly, glancing at the rock surround.

"*Gut!* Don't ever play around this well, Sam. It's dangerous here. If you ever fell inside, we'd never be able to find you."

"Caleb would *komm* find me," the boy claimed.

Tessa blinked. What on earth had possessed him to say that? The last thing she wanted was to rely on any man for protection, especially Caleb Yoder. Yes, she worked for the man, but she earned her keep. No one gave her any handouts. She was in charge of her own life and preferred it that way. What had happened yesterday in the park with Bryce Jackson only reconfirmed her desire to remain single. With her past, she didn't trust men easily—with good reason. That was why she fought so hard to become independent. It was best to teach her son self-reliance now. As far as she was concerned, asking others for help was a sign of weakness. It was better to push aside her fears and nip this idea in the bud. Right now.

Taking Sam gently by the arms, she turned him so he met her gaze. "*Ach*, you listen to me, Samuel Miller. We don't need to rely on anyone for help."

He stared at her with wide, uncertain eyes. "Not even Caleb?"

She shook her head. "Not even him. That's why we work so hard. We don't need anyone to rescue us. Not ever! We can take care of ourselves. You and me. Do you understand?"

He gave a little nod. "*Ja, Mammi.* It's like you always say...you and me are a team."

"That's right. You, me and *Gott*. We don't need anyone else." She hugged him again, so he wouldn't misunderstand and think she was angry with him. "Now, we better scurry."

Leaving the crumbling well behind, they hurried on their way. When they reached the main road, Tessa was startled as a horse and buggy pulled up beside them. Maybe they wouldn't be late for church after all.

"*Hallo!* Can we offer you a ride?" A woman waved as the buggy pulled over onto the shoulder of the road and stopped.

As she turned to face them, Tessa hid a surge of disappointment. Caleb and Doris sat looking at her. They wore their Sunday best. Though he wore a clean straw hat, Caleb's dark hair was still slightly wet from a washing and curled against his ears in damp waves. Of all the people in their *Gmay*, why did it have to be the Yoders who offered her and Sam a ride to church?

"*Guder mariye,*" Tessa called, forcing herself to be polite.

"Caleb!" Sam cried.

It was on the tip of Tessa's tongue to say she'd rather enjoy the beautiful day and walk, but Sam had already let go of her hand and sprinted toward the buggy. Besides, they were running very behind schedule.

As Tessa walked toward them, Doris opened the door and lifted the boy up.

"We just stopped by your apartment to offer you a ride, but you were already gone. *Komm* on. We don't want to be late for meetings." Doris beckoned.

Tessa stepped forward, surprised when Doris scooted into the back seat with Sam. That left the front passenger seat vacant for Tessa to sit next to Caleb.

Tessa floundered with indecision. Holding the leather lead lines in his big hands, Caleb leaned forward, watching her with expectation and a bit of impatience. From the scowl on his face, he wasn't any happier with this situation than she was.

Taking a deep inhale, she let it out slowly, knowing she would appear rude if she refused Doris's offer. Instead, she hopped up and closed the door. Setting her basket on the seat between them, she made a pretense of straightening her long, lavender skirt.

"This is so kind of you," she said before pressing her tongue into her cheek.

"*Ach*, it's no bother at all," Doris said.

Tessa tossed the woman a sweet smile. After all, she loved Doris.

Caleb slapped the leather against Tommy's rump, and the horse trotted forward. The buggy swayed as it was pulled onto the asphalt and headed on. Tessa could hear her son in the back, telling Doris about the decaying rock well they'd found.

"*Ach*, Caleb has been meaning to fill that old water well in for years. My husband's parents used to live there. *Dawdi* Nathaniel nailed boards over the top so no one would fall in. But my *kinder* and their friends were always playing in that field and pulled the boards off. The well is a hazard, that's for sure. Something really needs to be done about it," Doris said.

"I'll find the time to fill it in soon," Caleb promised, then glanced back at Sam. "But don't you play there, *allrecht*? It's dangerous."

Sam blinked, then nodded obediently. They rode in silence for several minutes. Tessa could hear Sam telling Doris how excited he was to see his friends and how he hoped they all could play baseball after church services.

Soon, Tessa saw the Burkholders' farm off in the distance. The red log home stood out like a beacon against the fields of green alfalfa. Off to the side, herds of black-and-white cows grazed peacefully. As the crow flew, it wasn't far to the house. Within minutes, they'd be pulling into the main yard. But if Tessa and Sam had continued to walk, they definitely would have arrived after the service had started.

"Are you recovered from the town fund-raiser yesterday?" Caleb asked quietly.

"*Ja*, I'm fine."

"*Du gucksht gut,*" Caleb said.

His praise that she looked good took her off guard. For a moment, she didn't know what to think or say.

"*Danke,*" she finally got out.

She stared straight ahead, not giving him any indication that she liked his compliment. She must not encourage this man. Because the moment she got close to him, he'd want to know who Sam's father was. And she couldn't tell him that. No, not ever.

* * *

A long row of buggies was parked along the outside fence bordering the Burkholder farm. Caleb pulled up, then hopped out to help Sam and the two women down. Two teenaged Amish boys came to unhitch Tommy and turn the animal out into a corral with the rest of the road horses.

"Caleb! Pick me up," Sam called.

He turned as the boy ran to him. Though this wasn't his child, Caleb couldn't resist Sam's endearing charm, and he clasped the boy beneath the arms and swung him up onto his shoulders.

"Look, *Mamm*! I'm taller than any of you," Sam crowed with delight.

Resting his hands beneath Caleb's chin to hold on, the boy made little galloping sounds, as if he was riding a horse. Caleb almost smiled.

Almost.

Tessa nodded and gave a wan smile before looking away. As Caleb walked with her and his mother toward the big red barn, he couldn't forget his promise to keep his distance from this woman. But Doris wasn't making things easy for him. Not when she had demanded they stop and give Tessa and Sam a ride.

"*Hallo*, Caleb!"

He looked up and saw Jonah Lapp and his wife and daughter. Their farm wasn't far away, and Caleb knew they must have walked here. Together, they all headed toward the barn.

"*Guder daag*," Caleb said, trying to be polite.

"You did a *gut* job with your food booth yesterday at the fund-raiser. I ate two hamburgers and a hot dog. Did you earn much for the town's new swimming pool?" Jonah asked.

"*Ja*, a tidy sum. How did you make out at the auction?" Caleb asked.

Jonah had been the auctioneer, rattling off quilt bids in a singsong voice that could have rivaled the best in the business.

"*Gut!* I'm sure the town will soon get their pool," Jonah said.

They had arrived at the long, graveled driveway leading up to the house. Caleb watched as Tessa's brother, Wayne, greeted her. Without asking, Caleb knew Wayne didn't approve of her living on her own. In their Amish community, it just wasn't done. A single woman and child normally stayed with her *familye* until she took a husband. That was just the way it was. And because it wasn't Caleb's business, he tried not to care. But he did and he didn't understand why.

"Well done on your new job, Tessa," Lovina Lapp said.

"*Danke,*" Tessa returned. Her lips curved upward just a bit, as if she was forcing herself to smile.

Hmm. Caleb wasn't surprised Lovina would congratulate Tessa. Lovina was their midwife and had lived on her own before she'd married Jonah. But even then, she'd had two caring men nearby if anything went wrong. Tessa and Sam were all alone. There was no way any of them could help her if there was a house fire or someone broke into her apartment and tried to hurt her and Sam. Never again did he want someone like Bryce Jackson to put his hands on Tessa. Caleb would rather die than see her hurt. And once more, that knowledge confused him.

As they reached the barn, Marva Geingerich's harsh voice sliced through the air. "I think it's terrible for a young woman of marriageable age to be living on her own with a small child."

At the age of ninety-three, Marva was the eldest matriarch in their *Gmay*. She'd been raised an Old Order Swartzentruber in Ohio and disapproved of almost everyone and everything. As she hobbled along with her wooden cane, she glanced at Tessa, then pursed her lips in disapproval.

"Caleb Yoder, you should stop this nonsense and marry Tessa and finally give Sam the father he deserves." Marva lifted her cane and jabbed it at Caleb for emphasis.

"With due respect, Marva, that's none of your business," he returned in as polite a voice as he could muster.

A gasp caused Caleb to turn. Tessa stood next to Lovina, her face drained of color. By this point, they had joined the crowd of Amish lining up outside the barn doors in preparation for going inside for Sunday services. Half of their congregation had overheard Marva's caustic jibe. From the mortified look on Tessa's face, she was devastated by the conversation.

Without a word, she whirled around and ran toward the back porch to the house. Since he'd been at this farm numerous times, Caleb knew the door led straight into the kitchen. Watching her go, Caleb felt the urge to go after her. She was hurt by their terse words, and he felt sorry. But there was no chance he would ever marry Tessa. Not after the way she'd broken his heart.

"*Ach*, Marva Geingerich, sometimes your barbed tongue is too cruel," Lovina said.

Marva drew herself up with indignation. "I don't know why you would say that. I just spoke the truth."

"What you said was unkind. The Savior taught us to love one another. I don't want Tessa to feel like an outsider among us. Do you?" Lovina's eyes were filled with challenge and outrage, and Marva looked away, seeming cowed for the moment. Without waiting for a response, Lovina hurried toward the house.

Looking at all the negative expressions turned her way, Marva relented just a bit. "Of course it's not what I want. But it needed to be said."

"*Ne*, it did not. It's not your place to be so judgmental." Doris tossed the older woman a disapproving frown and hurried after Lovina.

Good. Caleb's mom and Lovina would care for Tessa.

Though he turned away and tried to ignore the comments, he couldn't deny that he was upset, too. He didn't want a relationship with his ex-fiancée anymore, but neither did he want her hurt.

So, what did he want? He no longer knew.

"Caleb? Why is *Mammi* upset?" Sam asked from over Caleb's head.

As he set the boy on his feet, Caleb ruffled his hair. "Don't you worry. Your *mamm* is just fine. Now, why don't you go and join your friends? Service is about to start."

With a gentle push to Sam's back, he directed the tot

over to the other little boys. Watching him go, Caleb didn't think this was a conversation for a young, impressionable child. Except for this one big mistake, Tessa was a good woman. And Sam had a right to grow up respecting and thinking kindly toward his mother.

As he stepped inside the barn, Caleb inwardly shook his head. Sometimes, he didn't know what he wanted anymore. At one time, he'd longed to marry Tessa and raise a *familye* they both could cherish. But she seemed to want something else entirely. Against his will, Tessa had been brought in by his mother to work at the diner and live upstairs. Alone. With just her little boy. Then, Caleb had made the foolish decision to ask Tessa to work at his farm in the evenings, so Sam could learn agriculture and how to work with livestock. Then, yesterday, Caleb had stepped in to defend her when Bryce Jackson had hassled her. Rather than staying away from her, it seemed Caleb was being drawn into her world more and more. But marry her? Absolutely not!

In all honesty, he didn't know if he was coming or going. The only thing he knew was that he didn't trust Tessa. And if he let down his guard, he was going to find his heart shattered once more.

Chapter Seven

Over the next couple of weeks, Tessa quickly learned her jobs, both at the diner and at Caleb's farm. Other than a word or two, they shared very little interaction. He seemed to prefer it that way, but Tessa was worried about Doris. In spite of the extra chores Tessa had taken on, Doris never slowed down. Not even a little. On this particular morning, Tessa arrived at the diner extra early, even before Caleb got there.

Supporting her sleeping son on her hip with one arm, she unlocked the back door to the kitchen, but didn't turn on the light. Moving silently through the dark shadows, she laid Sam on the cot in the office and covered him with a blanket. The boy barely moved as she gazed at his serene face for several moments, letting her love fill her up for the busy day ahead.

Leaving the door slightly ajar in case he awoke, she returned to the kitchen and flipped on the light. She lathered her hands with hot soapy water, then reached for the large mixer. It was heavy, and she braced it against her chest as she set it on the worktable with a dull thud. Hopefully the noise of her chore wouldn't awaken her son.

In the quiet of the room, she moved around with ease, enjoying this peaceful time alone as she pulled out restaurant-size canisters of flour, yeast and sugar and a jug of oil. With her recipe nearby, she quickly filled a big measuring cup with warm water, added the appropriate amount of yeast and gave it a quick stir. Her nose twitched as the pungent aroma filled the air.

Leaving the mixture to activate, she dipped out the flour and other ingredients. Since she was making numerous loaves of bread, it took extra time to knead the gooey mass. Finally, she placed the soft, rounded balls of dough in an oiled container and covered them with a clean dishcloth while she greased the metal pans and set them aside. Leaving the dough to rise, she peeked in on her son, then hurried with her other chores. She'd just finished setting up the coffee makers when she heard a rattle and then a thump in the kitchen.

Caleb and Doris must be here.

Picking up her tray of salt and pepper refills, she hurried to the back. Doris was just hanging her wrap on the back of the door while Caleb tied his white chef's apron around his lean waist. Lifting the corner of one dishcloth, he peered at the rising bread dough, his forehead crinkled with curiosity.

"Guder mariye," Tessa called as she set her tray aside.

Caleb jerked in surprise and dropped the cloth.

"Tessa!" Doris exclaimed, her gaze scanning the worktable and making an obvious assessment. "You're here early. Making bread, I see."

Tessa nodded. "*Ja*, I hope that's okay. I wanted to help."

Doris smiled and wrapped one arm around her back for a quick hug. "Of course it's okay. You help us more than you'll ever know."

Caleb's heavy gaze rested on her with doubt. Tessa watched as Doris lifted one of the cloths to see how her efforts were working out. The full, elastic balls of dough told Tessa that her loaves were ready for putting into the pans.

"What lovely dough," Doris confirmed, tossing a nod at Caleb. "It looks like it's close to baking time."

"*Ja*, it should be almost done by the time we open for business," Tessa said.

"Yum! That'll make the restaurant smell delightful," Doris said.

With a nod, Tessa turned on the gas-powered oven. While it heated, she used her fists to punch the dough down, then quickly started shaping the balls into loaves before slapping them into the pans. As she worked, she was vaguely conscious of Caleb going about his own work. In her peripheral vision, she caught him glancing her way frequently, his eyebrows drawn together in a studious frown. Maybe he didn't like what she was doing. Maybe she had overstepped her bounds. Either way, his attention made her nervous, and her hands trembled slightly.

Doris hurried to wash her hands, then came to help. "Is Sam sleeping in the office?"

"*Ja*, we stayed up a little too late, and he seems overly tired. Even the sound of the mixer didn't disturb him this morning," Tessa said.

"*Gut!* Now that you've made the bread for me, I'll take him to the park after he's had his breakfast. *Danke* for doing this. I so appreciate it," Doris said.

Tessa smiled. At least the elderly woman was pleased by her efforts. But not Caleb, if his vexed frown was any indication.

"It's no trouble. I'm glad to do it," she said.

Together, the two women soon had eight loaves of bread rising for a second time in the pans.

"I'll clean up this mess," Doris said, reaching for the mixing bowl and measuring cups.

Tessa would have argued, but she glanced at the clock. Soon, it would be time to unlock the front door for business. Caleb and Doris were running late today.

"I'd rather you leave it for me," she said. "I can open the diner and then wash these dishes in between serving our customers."

"Nonsense! Then what would I do?" Doris asked.

"For starters, you could sit in the office and rest. Or, better yet, stay at home. Unless we have a busy patch, there's really no need for you to come to the diner at all," Caleb suggested.

Doris placed her hands on her waist and glared at him. "Humph! And who would look after little Sam all day?"

"We could take him to the farm to spend his days there with you. It'd be better for the child to stay at the farm than be cooped up here in the diner anyway," Caleb said.

Tessa agreed, but held her silence. This matter was between Caleb and his mom. But she couldn't help seeing the hurt look in Doris's eyes. Still, Tessa hoped the woman would listen to reason.

Doris shook her head. "I'm not about to sit around all day and be bored while you two do all the work. If I'm to do nothing at all, you might as well put me in the grave and pour the dirt over top of me right now. If it's my time to go, then so be it. But I'm not going to live a useless life in the meantime."

Caleb wisely didn't argue with his mom. Doris simply picked up the dirty dishes, carried them over to the sink, flipped on the faucet and put a giant squirt of dish detergent into the bowl. She wagged her hand around in the hot water to create lots of suds.

Tessa didn't argue, either, as she slid her loaves of bread into the oven and set a timer so she wouldn't forget. She understood Doris's reasoning and figured when she was older, she'd rather drop in harness, too. It'd be no fun sitting in a chair all day, being bored while life passed her by. She couldn't blame Doris for wanting to stay active. And yet, she understood Caleb's concerns for his mother, too.

"Tessa, it's time." Caleb jutted his chin toward the clock on the wall.

Feeling the friction between them, she hurried out into the dining room and pulled up the blinds, then flipped the Open sign around and unlocked the front door.

Through the window, she saw an elderly man wearing a beat-up cowboy hat, blue jeans and scuffed cowboy boots as he was getting out of his pickup truck. Planning to retrieve some ice water for him, Tessa rounded the counter when her nose caught the horrible stench of burning coffee.

Glancing at the coffee makers, she grimaced.

"Oh, *ne!*" she cried beneath her breath.

In all her activities that morning, she'd filled the machines with filters, coffee grounds and water but neglected to put the carafes beneath the drip spouts. The three glass decanters sat right where she'd left them—just to the side of the machines. As a result, hot coffee had spewed all over the countertop, down the front of the cabinets and onto the floor. As the liquid hit the warming plates, it sizzled and filled the room with an unpleasant stench.

Hurrying to snatch up a rag and dish tub, she started wiping up the mess.

"Tessa, I think something's burning..." Caleb came out of the kitchen and stepped over to the coffee makers.

He looked down, his mouth dropping open and his face contorting with shock as he realized he now stood in a puddle of hot coffee. Then he tossed her a dark look. He took a step toward Tessa, and a rush of absolute terror clawed at her throat. In a rush, a frightening memory of that horrible night zipped through her mind. Lifting her hands, she cowered in a corner.

Looking at her, Caleb blinked in surprise, then simply reached past her and turned off the machines.

She breathed out a gasp, realizing she had overreacted. This was Caleb. A man she'd known and loved most of her life. He might not like her, but he had never struck her. He had never even raised a hand of intimidation toward her. Her reaction made no sense. Even she didn't understand her frightened response.

"Are you *allrecht*?" he asked, looking startled and impatient at the same time.

"*Ja*. I... I'm sorry. I didn't mean for this to happen." She kept wiping up the mess in a frantic blur as Doris came out into the dining room.

"*Ach*, do I smell something burning?" she asked, her gaze sweeping over the scene with astute wonderment. "Oh, dear. What happened?"

Tessa heaved a weary sigh, not meeting the woman's gaze. It was obvious what had happened; she didn't need to explain. Using the dishcloth, Tessa soaked up hot coffee, then wrung it out in the tub again and again. Of all the ridiculous things she could have done. She'd simply forgotten to set the carafes in place so they could catch the pour of the hot liquid.

The bell over the door tinkled, and she knew the cowboy had finally come inside. Now was not the time to be cleaning up a big, stinky mess like this. And even worse, she now had no coffee to serve the cowboy.

A sense of urgency swept over her as she glanced up. Caleb had told her that nothing took precedence over serving their customers. Nothing.

She was prepared to abandon the mess in order to provide the cowboy with a menu. As she stood, she saw the man sniff the air, then crinkle his nose in repugnance as he frowned.

"Smells like you burned the coffee," he said, taking a seat in one of the booths lining the expansive windows.

"I'll take care of him. Don't worry. It's just a little

spilled coffee. No sense in being upset about it. We can quickly make a new batch." Speaking in *Deitsch*, Doris laid a consoling hand on Tessa's shoulder and squeezed gently before she stepped away.

Caleb didn't appear quite as understanding.

"You better get the mop," he growled low, handing her a clean dishcloth.

She flinched and hesitated before taking it. He tilted his head, looking alarmed.

"I think I'd better check your bread so it doesn't burn, too. Can you clean this mess on your own? Or do you need help?" he asked.

She heard the censure in his voice. The disapproval. She'd blown it big this time. He'd given her three months to see if she would work out, and now she feared he might fire her on the spot.

"*Ne*, I can do it." Her voice wobbled as she kept her head ducked over her chore.

Blinking back tears, she felt stupid, foolish and inept. She'd worked so hard to do something good today. So hard to take some of the burden off Doris. She'd hoped to earn Caleb's respect. And instead, all she'd done was make a big mess and disappoint him once again.

"Sam! What are you doing?" Caleb asked.

He'd just returned to the kitchen after Tessa's fiasco with the coffee makers and couldn't believe his eyes. Still dressed in his jammies, the child stood on a tall stool as he dumped flour and raw eggs into a big bowl sitting on the worktable. From the looks of things, Sam had poured more flour and eggs onto the table and floor than into the bowl.

"Hi, Caleb. I'm making pancake batter. I can help you make breakfast," Sam said, looking inordinately pleased with himself.

Snap!

Caleb whirled around as his mom placed an order into the holder. Normally, he arrived early at the diner and had bacon already cooked for the breakfast rush. Then all he had to do was warm it up. But *Mamm* had been running late, which made him late, too. And due to the coffee fiasco, he had nothing prepared. Now, Sam had made another mess to be dealt with. Caleb couldn't believe the chaos in his diner. If he didn't get a move on, he wouldn't have any soup to serve to the lunch bunch that usually came in around noon, nor would he have the salad bar set up.

"Sam! What are you doing?" Tessa came into the kitchen carrying the tub of coffee water and paused in the threshold.

The boy smiled wide. "I'm helping Caleb."

The front door tinkled, heralding a new arrival. Glancing through the cutout, Caleb saw a *familye* of five walk inside.

"Oh, dear!" Tessa exclaimed, hurrying over to her son. "Sam, what have you done?"

The boy looked up at her, his eyes filled with doubt. "I… I made batter."

The bread timer went off, its incessant beeping jangling Caleb's nerves even more. He hit the timer with his hand to shut it off, then reached for the oven mitts. A bolt of anger speared his chest. He'd hired Tessa to make life easier for him and *Mamm*, not to create more work. What did she think she was doing, bringing her son into his diner to make messes like this? If the health department came in to inspect the restaurant right now, he'd be hit with a huge fine.

As he pulled the oven door open, he turned his head aside as a rush of hot, fragrant air struck him in the face. At least the bread looked and smelled delicious. But the blast of heat infuriated him even more. In quick succession, he pulled the pans out and set them on the wooden block to cool. The tops of the bread were golden and lovely, the air filled with a delicious aroma. Tessa was definitely an excellent baker, but right now, they were open for business and the diner was in absolute chaos. And yet, getting mad at her and Sam wasn't going to resolve anything.

After turning off the oven, he stopped and gathered his emotions. He knew that both Tessa and Sam had tried to do something good today. It wouldn't help to get angry with them. And so, he laughed instead.

"*Ach!* We're sure having a fine day, aren't we?" he said, forcing a smile to his face.

Sam grinned from ear to ear and lifted his spoon in the air, flinging more batter against the floor in the process. "We sure are," the boy crowed with delight.

"Sam! Stop that." Tessa took the dripping spoon from her son's hand and set it on the counter.

Pushing aside his irritation, Caleb took a deep, calming inhale and glanced at Tessa. "If you can take care of Sam and clean up the messes, *Mamm* and I can wait on our customers. Once that's done, you can wait on tables while *Mamm* chops vegetables for a soup and salad bar. The day has gotten away from us, so we only have time for a pasta soup with a little celery and onion today."

"*Ja*, of course." She took hold of Sam and lifted him off the stool.

"But I wanna help. I can cut celery," the child cried as she set him on his feet. The boy broke away from his mother's grasp and ran over to Caleb.

"You need my help, don't you, Caleb?" Sam asked, his face filled with earnest desire.

Looking down at the boy, Caleb saw that Sam had a smear of flour across the bridge of his nose and a matting of egg yolk in his hair. He looked so eager to please. So earnest and guileless. His brown eyes were wide and filled with such hope. Eyes that Caleb didn't recognize. And for the umpteenth time, Caleb wondered when the boy's father might show up and take him and Tessa away. Why wasn't the guy here now, raising his son like a father should? Why hadn't he married Tessa and given her his name and protection? Caleb didn't understand. Not at all.

"Did I do something wrong?" Sam asked, his forehead creased with worry.

The anger melted out of Caleb. How could he be mad at this gentle, fatherless boy? None of this was Sam's fault. He was too young to know any better. But Caleb did. He had a choice to make, right then and there. He could scold Sam and damage the sweet relationship they had built. He could create resentment and anger in this child so that he grew up feeling inadequate and sad. Or, Caleb could praise Sam for his initiative and willingness to work and help build his self-esteem.

Conscious of Tessa standing beside her son, Caleb went down on his haunches and met Sam's gaze. He wiped the flour off the boy's nose and cleaned some of the goop out of his hair. Then, he cupped Sam's cheek with his hand and spoke in his calmest voice possible.

"It's *gut* that you want to help, Sam. But when you come into the kitchen, you've got to have an adult with you at all times. Because otherwise, I'll get into trouble with the health inspector. Do you understand why?"

Sam nodded, his eyes wide. "Is it because I'm still a little kid?"

"*Ja*, that's right. You're still a child. But one day, you'll be a fine, big man, and then you can do this all by yourself."

"But I wanna do it now," Sam whispered, his chin trembling slightly.

"I know, and you will. But not without an adult present. And later this afternoon, I'm going to let you assist me with making banana cream pies," Caleb said.

"Really?" Sam asked.

"*Ja*, really. But right now, I need you to go into the office and get cleaned up. You can't serve ice water to our customers in your pajamas. That wouldn't be right, now, would it?"

Sam looked down at himself, as if just realizing he was still in his jammies and bare feet. "Oh, *ne*! You're right. I've got to get dressed."

With no more incentive from his mother, the boy whirled around and dashed into the office. Ignoring Tessa, Caleb stood and checked the food orders, then reached for a package of bacon and a carton of eggs. Tessa hurriedly dumped Sam's flour mess into the garbage and placed the mixing bowl in the sink with the other dishes to soak. Then she reached for the mop and bucket. He glanced up as she paused before the door.

"*Danke* for that," she said.

"I didn't do it for you," he said.

She nodded and looked down, but not before he saw the deep, abiding sadness in her beautiful blue eyes.

"I know. But *danke* just the same. And I'm so very sorry for the trouble we've caused you today," she said.

And then she was gone, pushing the wheeled mop bucket out into the dining room.

In stiff motions, Caleb turned the eggs and bacon, then slapped some rye bread into the toaster to cook. He could hear Tessa on the other side of the wall, mopping up the floor. *Mamm* had restarted the coffeepots and was getting orange juice for their customers. Within twenty minutes, order was restored to the diner, and Doris returned to the kitchen to chop vegetables for later that day.

"Is everything *allrecht*?" she asked him as Sam joined them.

"*Ja*, let's just get through this day. Can you find some simple chore for Sam to do that will keep him out of trouble while we work?" Caleb asked as he slid two plates of food and a bowl of oatmeal underneath the warming lamps.

He spoke in English, a language Sam did not yet understand. The Amish spoke *Deitsch* in their homes, and children didn't learn English until they went to school at the age of five.

Out in the dining room, Tessa whisked the plates of food over to their customers. She moved quickly and efficiently, seeming to have regained her stride.

"Sure! Sam, why don't you stand on the stool right here next to me and separate these grapes from the vines? Then I'll let you help me wash them for the salad bar. And after that's done, I'll take you to the park," Doris said.

"Okay!" Sam smiled and started up a litany of his normal happy chatter.

Doris winked at Caleb, telling him that she had the boy well in hand. The orderly calm of the busy diner returned, and Caleb breathed a sigh of relief. But one quizzical feeling persisted in the back of his mind. Why had Tessa been frightened of him when he'd turned off the coffee machines?

As he flipped a row of pancakes on the grill in quick succession, he told himself once more that it wasn't his business. But none of her actions made sense. More than ever, he longed to know exactly what happened to Tessa all those years ago and what had induced her to forsake their love for a short fling with another man.

Chapter Eight

❦

"Order up!"

Tessa whipped her head around and glanced at the kitchen cutout. Six plates of food sat beneath the warming lights, waiting for her to shuttle them to the tables.

Holding a coffee carafe aloft, she refilled two more cups at table three, then headed toward the cash register so a customer could pay their bill. The teenaged girls sitting at table five erupted into peals of laughter. A low rumble of voices permeated the air from table eight. At nine o'clock on a Saturday morning, the restaurant was almost filled to capacity. Tessa was doing her best to keep up.

Sliding the near-empty carafe onto the hot plate, she quickly flipped up the lid to the machine, dumped the used filter and grounds into the garbage, slapped a clean filter in, added scoops of fresh coffee, then the water, and pressed the start button. Then she snatched up a wide, round tray and piled the plates of food on before hefting them over to table nine.

By the time she'd helped two more guests pay their

bills, taken the order for a *familye* of four and returned to the drink dispenser, she had a fresh pot of coffee ready to serve.

The bell over the front door tinkled, heralding more arrivals. Thankfully Sam was at the farm today with Doris. Caleb had finally convinced his mom to stay home for once. At least Tessa didn't have to worry about the older woman overdoing it or her son getting into trouble. But it also meant they were shorthanded.

She scanned the dining room, mentally noting she had one table empty that would seat four. As she reached for a pile of menus, she turned to greet the new customers...and her heart sank.

Bryce Jackson and two other *Englisch* cowboys she didn't recognize stood at the front counter, laughing and talking rather loudly. She hesitated. Would Bryce behave himself? He'd been inebriated that day in the park. Maybe he wouldn't even remember her.

"Good morning. How many in your party?" she asked politely.

Bryce turned and, as if in slow motion, she saw the recognition fill his eyes, and a silly grin crossed his face.

"Well, hi there, Tessa," he said, as if they were old friends.

Her body inwardly clenched in response. He took a step toward her, and she took one back. But not before she caught the pungent scent of liquor on his breath. She blinked, surprised by the man. It was still morning, yet he'd obviously been drinking already. Doris had told her he was an alcoholic. She couldn't fathom that. A part of her pitied him for the sadness in his life, while another part greatly disapproved of his weakness. Everyone had sadness in their life. Everyone had struggles and difficulties. But Caleb had made it clear that happy customers were their number-one priority. So, she pasted a smile on her face.

"We've got three in our party. Ain't that right, Charlie?" One of the men jabbed his friend with his elbow.

Charlie flinched but laughed raucously. "Yeah, we got three, but we could make it four, if you'd join us."

She didn't respond to that. What she wanted to do was tell the men to get out and never come back. But Caleb wouldn't like that. He'd given her three months to see if she could do well here, and she didn't want to give him another excuse to fire her. Instead, she waved a beckoning hand and simply headed toward the vacant table.

"If you'll follow me, please," she said.

Crude laughter came from behind her, but she didn't look.

"I'll follow you anywhere, honey."

That was Bryce's voice, filled with innuendo. Tessa inwardly cringed, and a flush of heat filled her face with embarrassment. Forcing herself not to turn around, she could see other customers glancing her way. No doubt they'd overheard the comment and wondered about her. Instead of acknowledging Bryce's words, she navigated through the restaurant, then stood aside as she waited for the cowboys to take their seats.

"Would you like something to drink?" she asked as she slid a menu in front of each man.

"Coffee for me," Charlie said, waving a hand in the air.

She nodded, then looked at the next man. He set his beat-up cowboy hat on the empty seat beside him and smiled wide. But before she could get his order, Bryce reached across the table and took hold of her wrist. She pulled back, but was no match for his greater strength. Against her will, she found herself being propelled onto Bryce's lap as he tugged her down.

"Let go!" she cried out before she could stop herself.

"Ah, why don't you join us, honey? You've been working hard. You need a little break," he said.

A feeling of absolute terror overwhelmed her, and she struggled to be free. "Please! Let me go!"

Before she knew what was happening, she found herself being pulled free.

"Excuse me, but Tessa is needed in the kitchen."

Slightly off balance, she turned and fell headfirst against Caleb's solid chest. He stood beside the table, wearing his clean white chef's apron, the long sleeves of his shirt rolled up on his muscular forearms. As she stumbled, he clasped her upper arms to steady her, and she stared up at him in surprise. A feeling of relief flooded her mind. She'd never been so happy to see him in all her life.

"Go into the kitchen and cook the food. I'll wait on the tables until these men leave." He spoke in *Deitsch* so no one but her understood.

Pressing his solid palm against the middle of her back, he pushed her gently in that direction, then faced the three rowdy cowboys.

"So, what can I get you gentlemen to drink?" he asked pleasantly in perfect English.

Bryce tried to follow Tessa, but Caleb stood so close

that the cowboy couldn't stand up straight and plunged back onto his chair.

"Hey! I wanted Tessa to wait on us. What's that you said to her, anyway?" Bryce grouched.

Caleb chuckled behind her, seeming to sound amiable. But Tessa caught the edge of irritation in his voice.

"Oh, nothing important," Caleb said. "She's got work to do in the back area. Would you like coffee or juice this morning?"

Tessa zipped around the corner and didn't hear Bryce's response, but she knew Caleb was doing his best to distract the three men without using any force. She reached the kitchen and quickly assessed where they were in terms of food prep. A scan of the orders she'd written out gave her a new perspective. Though she'd never assumed the role of cook before, she knew the lay of the land and immediately considered what must be done.

Moving fast, she slapped slices of whole wheat bread into the toaster, then cracked three eggs into a bowl. She whisked them with a bit of milk and cubed ham and cheese for an omelet. As she reached for the pancake batter to dribble onto the grill, her hands trembled and her legs wobbled. It felt like she was reliving that night of horror five years earlier all over again. But there wasn't time to be upset right now. The diner was filled to capacity, and Caleb was counting on her. He needed her help.

"Are you *allrecht*?"

She jerked and glanced at the cutout. Caleb snapped up another order, but didn't turn away immediately.

Her gaze locked with his for several pounding moments.

"Are you okay?" he asked again, speaking in *Deitsch*.

She nodded. "*Ja, danke.* I'm fine."

But she wasn't. Not really.

He stepped over to the coffee maker, but not before she saw a tinge of concern in his eyes. The fact that he had protected her without physically fighting did not escape her recognition. He glanced at the table where Bryce and his two friends were laughing and gesturing a bit more than they should in polite circumstances. And in that moment, Caleb's expression changed to smoldering anger. Whether he was angry at her or Bryce, Tessa wasn't sure. She was beyond grateful for what Caleb had done, but what if he decided she was more trouble than she was worth? She didn't want to lose this job. Not now, when she finally had a chance at independence.

She briefly considered telling him the truth about what happened to her in Denver five years ago. It might help him understand. Or it could backfire on her, too. He might get rid of her out of pure disgust.

She couldn't take the chance. No one must ever know the truth, especially Sam. Everyone in her *Gmay* wondered about her already. Some had even asked about Sam's father. Who he was. Where he lived. Why he wasn't here taking care of his son. If they found out the truth, someone might tell Sam. One day, when he was older, somebody might let the truth slip out. And how could she explain to her precious little boy that he'd been the result of violence? She didn't want to hurt him. Not like that. Who his father was didn't matter.

Not to her. Sam was her son, and she cherished him. That was all she wanted him to ever know. Like always, she would gather her faith and courage around her and keep her silence. She was truly alone in the world, with no one but *Gott* to fully rely on. Never would she tell a single soul what had happened to her. Not ever. Most especially not Caleb Yoder.

What was wrong with Tessa? Caleb didn't know. He'd been working in the kitchen, feverishly trying to keep up with the continual orders. It was the weekend of the Fourth of July, and everyone in town seemed to have descended on his diner. That was good. In fact, it was stupendous. Business was their lifeblood. He would never complain about being too busy. And he'd been more than impressed by how Tessa kept up with the flow. Like a pro, she'd ferried food to the tables, brewed more coffee, filled drinks and delivered setups to each customer in a timely fashion. She wasn't just doing well. She was doing a fantastic job. And once the day was over with, he planned to tell her so…

Then, Bryce Jackson and his rowdy friends had come into the diner. From the cutout, Caleb had seen the men standing by the door before Tessa had, and all his senses went on high alert. Even before Bryce spotted her, Caleb instinctively knew the cowboy was a problem waiting to happen. And they didn't need trouble on such a busy day.

Making a quick decision, Caleb had cleared the grill so nothing would burn and stepped out into the restaurant to retrieve Tessa. It'd be better if she worked in the back until Bryce and his friends left. And then Bryce had pulled her onto his lap.

Something wild and furious had risen upward inside Caleb's chest. Who did Bryce think he was, manhandling Tessa that way? Caleb knew *Gott* wouldn't approve of fighting. In fact, he could be shunned by his Amish people for doing such a thing. And so, he'd clenched his hands, forced himself to calm down and used his wits instead.

When Tessa had fallen against him, Caleb had seen the shock and horror in her eyes. He'd steadied her and told her to go into the kitchen. Thankfully, she'd swiftly done as he asked. But just like that day in the park when they'd provided food for the town fundraiser, she'd seemed overly traumatized by what happened. And once again, Caleb wondered why.

Hmm. He'd told himself it wasn't his business. That he didn't really care. But he knew that wasn't true. He cared. Very much. And that was just the problem. He didn't want to worry about Tessa and her sweet little boy. But maybe he should ask her about it one more time. Maybe he should try to understand what was going on with her.

Retrieving a dish tub, he quickly cleared a table so he could seat some more guests. He caught the whiff of burning toast and glanced toward the kitchen. Through the cutout, he saw a thin stream of smoke as Tessa frantically pulled a blackened piece of bread out of the toaster.

He thought about going to help her, but decided against it. Bryce would undoubtedly return to the diner again and again as time went by. And if he did, Tessa would go work in the kitchen. She'd need to know what to do in there. She'd learn fast by handling her mistakes on her own.

Instead, Caleb kept waiting on the tables. Bryce and his cronies languished in the diner for over two hours. And when they left, Caleb glanced around the dining room and realized the rush had finally died off. He figured he had just enough time to help Tessa wash the dishes and get the salad bar assembled before the lunch rush hit.

Stepping into the kitchen, he saw her standing at the prep sink, rinsing bunches of radishes. With her back to him, he was able to study her posture for several moments. She was nimble and worked fast and efficiently, the cool, clear water rushing over her hands. But her spine and shoulders were tense, and she kept glancing through the cutout. She lifted her hand and wiped her brow with her forearm. Her fingers visibly trembled, and he knew she was distraught. And though he didn't fully understand the cause, he was impressed by how she'd pushed aside her own anxieties and kept on working.

"Tessa."

She turned, her forehead creased with surprise. Seeing him, her expression relaxed and she turned back to her chore.

"*Ach*, Caleb. Have those men left yet?" she asked.

A feeling of compassion rose up inside his chest. "They have. You can go back out now. I've got this."

She set her coring knife aside and dried her damp hands on a dish towel. "Has it finally slowed down a bit?"

"*Ja*, but I believe it'll pick up again in an hour or so when people get hungry for their noon meal."

She nodded and stepped toward the door. He reached out and touched her arm, stopping her.

"Tessa, if those men *komm* into our place again, I don't want you to even acknowledge them. You just skirt around the front counter and *komm* right in here to the kitchen and get me. I'll go out and wait on the tables while you cook. Later, when we aren't so busy, I'll show you a few things to help teach you what to do in here. I don't want you to have to deal with those men again. It's better if I handle them instead. Understood?" he asked.

She nodded, darting a wary glance toward the front door, as if she thought she might see Bryce Jackson standing there right now.

"What's going on with you?" Caleb asked, trying not to disturb her by posing too many questions.

She wouldn't meet his gaze. "I... I don't know what you mean."

He jutted his chin toward the dining room. "Bryce upsets you a lot. I know he's a rude, unruly man, but he's harmless enough. Yet you look so frightened whenever he's around. I'm just trying to understand why."

She tried to sidle past him. She'd rolled her sleeves up past her elbows so she could wash dishes. He touched her arm again, finding her skin soft and warm beneath his palm. She looked at his fingers and frowned. He let her go.

"I'm grateful for what you did today. But I could have handled it myself," she said.

He doubted it, but didn't say so. When she'd looked at him, her eyes had been filled with absolute horror. If he hadn't stepped in, he had no idea what might have happened. And what's more, he didn't want to find out.

"I wish you'd talk to me. We were close friends once and confided in each other. You used to tell me everything," he said.

And he'd done the same with her. Then she'd gone off to Denver and met someone, and nothing had been the same ever since.

"I... I have nothing to tell you. I need to get to work."

She all but ran out to the dining room. He stood there watching her go, listening to her pile dirty dishes in a tub as she cleared the tables. What was going on? Why wouldn't she talk to him?

His mind scanned the myriad conversations they'd had over the many years they'd known each other. He couldn't think of one single thing he'd said that might have driven her into the arms of another man. In fact, the last thing he'd told her the day before she went to Denver was that he loved her. She'd responded that she loved him, too. And that, when she returned, they'd finally set the date for their wedding. They'd be baptized into their faith first and married a week later. Their lives were all planned and entwined together. Inseparable. Everything revolved around each other.

So, what had happened in the span of those four days while she was gone? What had she done? Where had she gone? Whom had she met?

He couldn't fathom it. Couldn't make sense of anything. She'd hurt him so deeply. She'd crushed his heart and destroyed his trust in love. Now, he was stuck in limbo and didn't know which way to turn. He sensed that she needed help, but he was at a loss what to do. His sympathy for her warred with his anger. They'd been crazy about each other, and look what she'd done. And as it stood right now, he didn't believe there was anything Tessa could say to him that would ever make things right between them again.

Chapter Nine

❧

Tessa awoke slowly and rolled onto her side. Blinking her eyes open, she stared into the darkness of night. In the moonlight gleaming through the open window of her bedroom, she peered at the clock. It was just after midnight. So, what had awoken her?

Someone pounded on her front door. She sat straight up and opened her eyes wide. Who was here at this late hour?

Sliding out of bed, she pulled her bathrobe tight around her. Making her way across the hall, she peeked in at Sam, finding him sound asleep. She pulled his door closed, then went into the main living room.

The thumping came again. She stepped over to the door, leaning close as she listened intently. Someone was there. But who?

"Tessa, are you in there, honey? Let me in!"

Bryce Jackson!

She reared back and clasped a hand over her mouth to keep from screaming. What was the man doing here? What did he want?

He knocked again and again. When she didn't respond, he pounded harder, which told her he was using his fist.

"Let me in, Tessa," Bryce called, slamming against the door, as if he was ramming his shoulder against the portal to break it in.

Prickles of alarm flooded her body. As a pacifist, she knew it was wrong to fight back. But neither was she going to open the door to him. At one time, she thought she'd rather die than defy the tenets of her faith and use force to protect herself from someone like Bryce. But that was before she'd gone to Denver. Before she had Sam to protect...

Her son's baseball bat sat in a corner by the door. He frequently had it with him when Doris took him to the park to play. Reaching for it, Tessa clasped the handle with both hands and lifted it high. She stood there silently, not knowing what to say or do. Not daring to speak. But if Bryce broke into her home, she would...

"Mammi?"

She turned. Sam stood right behind her. Her heart sank. She didn't want her son to be hurt or afraid. Nor did she want him to see her like this.

Reaching for him, she picked him up and hurried to her bedroom. Closing the door, she placed her son in the middle of her bed, then pushed and shoved until the heavy chest of drawers sat in front of the portal. Praying the front dead bolt held against Bryce's force, she set the bat nearby and crawled under the covers with her son, holding him close.

"Mammi, who is that at our door?" Sam whispered,

peering up at her with wide eyes. He seemed to sense her desire to remain quiet.

"It's nobody. They'll go away. Everything will be *allrecht*. Just go to sleep now," she said, speaking low enough that she hoped Bryce wouldn't hear her.

"Maybe we can hide in the well," Sam returned.

Tessa frowned. "The well?"

Oh, she really didn't want to have this conversation right now.

"*Ja*, the old abandoned water well in Caleb's field. You said no one would ever find me there. We could hide real good."

She gripped her son's slender shoulders. "*Ne*, don't you ever hide in that well. It's dangerous, *sohn*. Do you understand me?"

He gave a solemn nod, but didn't reply.

The knocking persisted for a few minutes more. Then, all went very quiet. Blessed, peaceful silence. Bryce must have gotten the message and left. Thank the Lord.

Tessa lay there, very still. Sam soon relaxed against her, and she knew he slept. But it was a long time before she dared relax. The hours passed, and finally she crept out of bed, slid the chest of drawers aside and stepped out into the living area. There was no more pounding on her door. No slurred requests to come inside.

Bryce was truly gone. His actions had resurrected dark memories for her, but he'd been unsuccessful in breaking into her home.

But what if he returned? What must she do? Above all else, she would protect her son. Never, ever would she allow him to be hurt. Even if she must use the baseball bat and be forever shunned by the members of her *Gmay*, she would never let anyone harm her child.

She returned to her bed and closed her eyes. Finally, she lost consciousness. And when she awoke with a jerk, she discovered it was morning and she'd overslept.

"Sam?" she called, searching for him.

She hurried across the hall to his room. His bed had been made in a haphazard, childlike manner. And from the jammies she found on the floor, she could tell he'd gotten dressed already. She smiled, thinking what a good boy he was and how blessed she was to have him.

But where was he?

Dashing to the front door, she saw the dead bolt had been unlocked. She looked out on the landing, frantic to find her boy. No one was there. A car zipped past on the street below, the town just starting to come to life.

Racing back to her room, she dressed and then hurried downstairs to the diner. She should have been here over half an hour earlier. Just one more infraction that might convince Caleb to fire her.

Desperate to find her son, she dashed inside the kitchen and paused. Sam stood on a high stool, happily stirring what looked like pancake batter. Caleb stood in front of the cutting board, dicing celery and onion. At her entrance, he looked up.

"*Guder mariye.* I was wondering when you might get here," he said.

She caught a hint of censure in his voice. He smiled as he returned to his work. If he fired her now, she wouldn't argue one bit. Maybe it was best for her to return to Wayne's farm. Though she'd be a burden on her brother and his wife for the rest of her life, at least Sam would be safe. That was all that mattered.

Stepping over to the counter, she smoothed her son's hair, noticing it hadn't been combed properly.

"You mustn't leave the apartment without me, *liebchen*. I was worried about you," she told him.

"Why?" he asked, his eyes filled with innocent curiosity.

She opened her mouth to explain, but noticed Caleb was watching them closely. She didn't want to make her son afraid, but neither did she want him to run off like this again.

Using her motherly voice, she kept her tone even but firm. "Because…because I didn't know where you were. You need to ask me first. Then I won't be afraid. *Allrecht?*"

Sam shrugged. "Okay. I'll tell you next time, *Mamm*."

They were interrupted when Doris came from the back office. The woman gave her usual cheery smile.

"*Hallo*, Tessa. I've already filled the salt and pepper shakers for you. I hope you're not getting overly tired with your work here," she said.

"*Ne*, I… I'm sorry I'm late today," Tessa said.

Doris beckoned to Sam. "*Komm* on. It's time for us to go to the farm."

"*Ach*, do I have to? I wanna help Caleb make pancakes," the boy grumped.

Doris picked up a jar with a lid on it. "You can help me make pancakes at *heemet*. I've got some batter right here just for your breakfast."

Sam hopped down off the stool. "Okay."

They headed toward the door, but Tessa called the child back.

"What about my kiss and hug?" she said.

Sam ran into her open arms, pressed his lips to her cheek and grunted as he squeezed her extra hard. And then he was off.

Watching him go, Tessa thought she'd never loved anyone more…except for Caleb, long ago.

The back door clapped closed behind them. Tessa knew they would walk the few blocks to Caleb's farm. She was grateful her son had a fun, safe place to spend his day.

As she looped her blue apron over her head and tied it behind her back, she glanced at Caleb. He stood watching her, a peculiar frown crinkling his forehead. His eyes were filled with disapproval, and she realized she may have tested his patience too much this time.

"You look tired today," he said.

"I… I'm fine."

"I think we should talk."

Turning to face him, she took a deep inhale and let it out slowly. Here it was. The moment when he would fire her, with good reason.

Resting a hand on the doorjamb to steady herself, she mentally prepared her mind to accept his justice. And deep in her heart, she thought perhaps it was for the best. If she was back on her brother's farm, she wouldn't be exposed to men like Bryce Jackson. She and Sam would be safe again. But she wouldn't be able to see Caleb anymore. Their lives would return to what they'd been for several years now, with her seeing him only on church Sunday or at special gatherings. But at that moment, she hated that she had disappointed Caleb once more.

"I… I really should get to work now," Tessa said, turning toward the dining room.

"Tessa, wait."

She hesitated, finally turning to meet his gaze. There were dark circles beneath her eyes, and her face looked drained of color. The weary slump of her shoulders looked to be caused more by defeat than fatigue. And he hated seeing her this way. Hated that anyone might ever do her harm.

"Did you sleep poorly last night?" he asked, wishing she would confide in him. Wishing she would tell him everything that had happened to her in the past.

"I did, but I'm fine now. Truly, it won't impact my work. I promise," she said, sounding slightly anxious and…

Desperate.

He grunted, looking away. Trying to appear casual and unperturbed. The last thing he wanted was to scare her off or upset her more.

"I understand you had an unexpected visitor on your doorstep late last night," he said.

Her eyes widened, and she licked her upper lip, fidgeting with her hands. "Did Sam tell you that?"

He nodded. "He said a bad man was pounding on your door in the middle of the night. Was it Bryce Jackson?"

She hesitated, as if she didn't want to tell him about it. Finally, she nodded.

"What happened?"

She shrugged. "He beat on the door. We ignored him. I didn't even speak to him. Pretty soon, he went away. I took Sam and we went back to bed. And that was it," she said.

Hmm. Interesting how she omitted that she'd barricaded her bedroom door with the heavy chest of drawers. At least, that was what Sam had told Caleb.

"Okay, as long as no harm was done. Are you sure you're okay?" he asked, watching her face carefully. Searching for any signs of the panic he'd seen there each of the other times when Bryce had hassled her.

She turned away, busying herself with picking up the empty bread baskets. He knew she would fill them with clean napkins in preparation for use later in the day.

"*Ja*, we're both fine. There's no need for you to worry. I handled it on my own," she said.

Without further comment, she hurried out into the dining room. Watching her go, Caleb realized it was highly important to her that she deal with this problem herself. And yet, he feared she was in way over her head. As pacifists, they didn't believe in physical aggression. But neither could Caleb stand by and watch as Bryce badgered a defenseless Amish woman and her young child.

Scooping up handfuls of chopped onion and celery, he dumped them into the soup pot before setting it on the stove to simmer. Bryce seemed to take particular delight in harassing Tessa. It was one thing for him to do that in the park or here at the diner, where there were numerous other people around. But for the man to actually go to Tessa's apartment in the middle of the night—that was something else entirely. The guy was usually inebriated and not in his right mind. So, what if things escalated out of control? Would Bryce hurt Tessa or Sam? Caleb didn't want to find out. But what should he do about it? That was the big question he was struggling with right now.

Hmm. Maybe Caleb should talk to the police. He hated involving the *Englisch* authorities in their affairs. Not without first consulting Bishop Yoder, the leader of their Amish community. And he hated the thought of doing that, because it would only increase the gossip surrounding Caleb and Tessa. But this was becoming a serious problem.

Caleb thought when Bryce bothered Tessa at the town fund-raiser, it was a onetime thing. Then, when the man had troubled her right here in the diner, Caleb figured they had nipped the problem in the bud and found a good solution for future encounters. But Bryce going to her apartment and pounding on her door in the middle of the night was too much. Tessa had brushed it off, like it was no big deal and didn't matter. But Caleb knew her too well. The subtle shifting of her feet, the anxious way she twined her fingers together and the furtive way she avoided meeting his gaze when he asked her about it told him everything. No matter what she said, he could tell she was upset about the situation. It was a big deal. And Caleb was determined to do something about it.

But what?

Chapter Ten

Tessa lifted the heavy black bag out of the trash can, then leaned her weight on it to smash the garbage down and force excess air out. Though it was full, it wasn't overly heavy. With a quick turn of her hand, she secured the top with a twist tie and carried it to the back door. They'd closed the restaurant over two hours earlier. The summer sunshine gave them longer days, but it was almost nine o'clock and evening shadows shrouded the open window where a gentle breeze flickered the curtains. Sam had fallen asleep on the cot in the back office. She wasn't eager to retrieve him and go home to her lonely apartment, but it was time to put him in bed.

After peeking into the alley to ensure no one was skulking there, she stepped out and lifted the lid to the big green dumpster. Tossing the refuse inside, she stepped away and took a deep, cleansing breath, then stood against the redbrick wall for a moment. Her hands were shaking. Again. Throughout the day, she'd feared Bryce Jackson might come into the restaurant and hound her. Now, she dreaded going up to her apartment, where she'd be alone with Sam. As she'd wracked her wits for a strategy to deal with the man, a plan had formulated in her mind. It would be difficult, but she would place the heavy chest of drawers from her bedroom in front of the living room door each night. She couldn't prevent Bryce from coming to her doorstep, but she would do everything in her power to keep him from getting inside her apartment.

"What are you doing?"

She whirled around. Caleb stood in the open doorway. He'd been working late, too, catching up on the accounts Doris had left for him to review. He glanced her way as he pulled his chef's apron over his head and crumpled it in a tight fist.

"I… I just dumped the garbage," she said, indicating the big dumpster.

He wore a quizzical expression. "It's late, and Sam's sound asleep in the office. Would you like me to carry him up to your apartment for you?"

They'd eaten their supper over an hour ago, but she kept finding excuses to linger in the restaurant. Scrubbing the toilets and sinks, mopping the floors, cleaning the silverware bins. Anything to avoid going upstairs. It was a slow night, so Caleb had ducked out earlier to do their farm chores while she kept an eye on the diner. She needed to go home now.

"Um, *ne*. I'll get him." She brushed past Caleb and stepped into the kitchen.

Inside the office, she picked up her son and cradled him against her hip. The boy barely stirred as his head slumped against her shoulder. Caleb followed and sat at the desk, where he picked up a pencil and notebook.

"Gut nacht," she said.

Caleb grunted but barely glanced her way. She hesitated a moment, briefly considering the consequences of asking him to accompany her. In her heart of hearts, she wished he would ensure there was no one lurking inside her apartment. If she asked, Caleb would check for her, but he'd then realize how frightened she really was. And she couldn't bring herself to reveal that weakness to him. Not now. Not after everything she'd put him through.

In the fading light, she hurried up the steep flight of stairs. Struggling not to drop Sam, she unlocked the door, stepped inside and quickly threw the dead bolt. After laying her son on the sofa, she made a swift but exhaustive search of the entire apartment to ensure they were alone, then returned and took Sam to bed. The boy released a soft sigh as she covered him with a blanket, and she gazed at him for several minutes, letting his sweet face soothe her jangled nerves. Then she set to work.

It took a lot of effort and a little time, but she pushed and shoved until the heavy chest of drawers blocked the front door. Heaven help her if they had a house fire. She would never be able to move the heavy furniture in time for a quick exit. But at least they were secure in case Bryce returned. Though she was trying hard to be strong and independent, she had never felt more frightened and alone.

She retrieved a pillow and blanket from her bed and laid down on the couch, shifting and turning on the lumpy cushions. Finally, she drifted off, though she never fully lost consciousness. She wavered in that nether region between fretful wakefulness and utter exhaustion. Not fully awake but not quite asleep. She jerked when someone pounded on her front door.

Springing to her feet, Tessa peered through the dark shadows. Brandishing his baseball bat, Sam ran into the living room and scurried over to her.

"*Mammi!* Who is that?" he cried, his eyes wide with fear.

She took the bat from him, then pushed him behind her as the knock came again. She didn't answer, because, honestly, she was too afraid. A glance at the clock on the wall told her it was almost eleven thirty. Not as late as she thought.

"Is it the bad man again?" Sam whispered loudly as he pressed against her side.

"Hush, *liebchen*. Everything will be *allrecht*," she quieted him.

The knock came again. "Tessa, it's Caleb. Are you okay?"

Caleb! A flood of relief washed over her. She'd never been so happy to hear his voice in all her life.

"*Ja*, I'm here. Just a minute."

Tossing the bat onto the couch, she pushed and shoved to move the chest of drawers enough to open the door. Caleb stepped inside, glancing at the heavy furniture with a dubious frown. Sam immediately launched himself at the man.

"Caleb! I'm so glad you're here," Sam said.

The man picked up Sam and smiled. "Hi, buddy. I wanted to see if you and your *mudder* are doing okay."

Sam's expression turned quite sober. "I'm doing great, but I think *Mammi* was worried."

Caleb glanced her way. He took in the baseball bat and the fact that she was still fully dressed in her work clothes…shoes and all. Then he eyed the dresser again. And she could see from his expression that he knew exactly what she'd done. A flicker of amusement crossed his face, and his eyes sparkled with laughter. And suddenly, she laughed, too. Because, when she really thought about it, her actions must look ridiculous.

"Did you move that all the way in here from your bedroom?" he asked.

She lifted her chin higher in the air. "*Ja*, I did."

He released a low chuckle. "You always were a spunky little thing."

She snorted, no longer amused. After all, she'd been scared to death when he'd pounded on her door. "It's not funny. Not really."

He took a step. "*Ach*, if we don't find humor in the moment now and then, there's little joy in life. Don't you agree?"

She did but wouldn't admit it right now. Instead, she pursed her lips. "Was there something you wanted at this late hour? You should be home by now. Doris will be worried about you."

"Tessie, don't be angry. I just wanted to know that you and the boy were safe before I headed *heemet*," he said.

Tessie! He hadn't called her that name in years. And hearing the genuine concern in his voice almost undid her. She nearly burst into tears right then and there. She longed to confide in him. To tell him everything about her past and share her sordid secret with someone she could trust. But that was just the problem. She couldn't trust him, or anyone. Not now. Not ever again. The cost was too high.

"*Ja*, we're fine. I was just making us safe by moving the dresser in front of the door. Just in case you-know-who returns," she said.

Okay, a teeny bit of truth wouldn't hurt.

"You mean Bryce Jackson?" Sam asked, his little nose crinkled with repugnance. "If he comes here, I'll hit him with my baseball bat," the boy said.

Tessa gasped. "You will not. Jesus taught that we should never return evil for evil."

"But what if he hurts us first?" Sam asked, his forehead furrowed.

"Then he will hurt us. But we must exhibit *gelassenheit* and show a humble yielding to *Gott*'s will, no matter what," she said, fighting against her own desire to strike back. Teaching her son what she believed helped bolster her faith and reconfirm her desire never to use aggression, no matter what. But it wasn't easy.

"Your *mudder* is right. We must shun all violence and turn the other cheek at all times. We must trust in the Lord." Caleb set Sam on his feet, then shrugged one shoulder. The fear must have shown on her face, because he took a step closer and leaned his head down to peer through the darkness into her eyes.

She turned away. "As you can see, we're just fine. *Komm* on, Sam. I'll take you back to bed."

Reaching for her son's hand, she led him into his room. Caleb followed, standing tall in the doorway as she tucked the boy beneath the covers and kissed his cheek. Then she closed his door and returned with Caleb to the living room.

"You don't look *allrecht*." Caleb spoke from behind her.

"We are," she insisted, opening the door wide in invitation for him to leave.

He pursed his lips and shook his head. "Uh-uh. I'm not buying it."

Great! He knew what a coward she was. She could see it in his eyes.

"You didn't need to check on us," she said.

"I'm concerned about you. I always have been."

Ah, that hurt. Because she didn't deserve his consideration. Not after everything she'd done to hurt him.

"You're right. I… I was too afraid to sleep, that's all. Are you happy now?" She blurted out the words before she could pull them back. "But I've got to protect Sam. That's all that matters. He's traumatized enough by Bryce Jackson—and you, pounding on our door in the middle of the night. No matter what, I'll never let anyone brutalize my son the way I was—"

She bit her lip to stop herself from saying more. The words had burst from her mouth in a rush. Anxiety and sleep deprivation had taken their toll. She wasn't thinking clearly and had said too much.

"Brutalized? What do you mean?" Caleb asked, his forehead crinkled in confusion.

Oh, dear. Now he was suspicious. But he must never know the truth. She didn't want to stigmatize her son. Nor did she want to lose her job because Caleb thought she was too much trouble to work at the diner. She also hated the thought of returning to her brother's house.

"Nothing. I don't mean anything at all. Thanks for checking on us. And now, it's late. You should go *heemet*. We've got a busy day tomorrow." She gently but insistently pushed against his arm, urging him toward the door, hoping he would take the hint.

"I'll go, but I'm not leaving. I'll get the cot from downstairs in the office and sleep outside on your doorstep tonight," he said, stepping out onto the landing above the stairs.

She gasped, her cheeks heating up like road flares. A part of her was deeply touched that he would put aside his own comfort for her and Sam. Another part was absolutely outraged.

"*Ne!* You can't sleep here tonight. Imagine what people would say if they found out," she said.

He faced her, his broad chest and shoulders filling her view. A streetlight gleamed from the real estate office next door. In the shadows, his cheeks seemed sharper and sterner than ever before.

"Let them talk. I'm more concerned with your and Sam's safety. We'll talk about possible solutions to this problem tomorrow. Now, close and bolt the door behind me and don't open it again until morning. Understand?"

Without another word, he turned and pounded down the stairs. She would have argued the point, but he was long gone. Standing there in the dark, she took a deep inhale, conscious of the warm night air enfolding her trembling body. She hunched her shoulders as she folded her arms.

She did as Caleb instructed and went back inside before locking the door. After she'd checked on her son once more, she returned to the living room and heard the unmistakable rattle of Caleb setting up the cot on the landing. It was a beautiful summer night, so he should be able to sleep okay. A part of her was relieved to have him here. For the first time in a long time, she felt safe. But then, something hardened inside her. She couldn't live in fear like this. Not indefinitely. If she was going to retain her independence, she must be able to work and care for herself and Sam. And if Bryce Jackson injured her, she must accept it as *Gott*'s will.

But what about Sam? She couldn't let Bryce hurt her son. No, not ever. Not even if it meant she'd be shunned by her people.

She had to figure something out. And soon. She didn't want to lose her job or have to return to her brother's farm and live off his generosity the rest of her life. That would deaden her heart. Nor could she allow Caleb to sleep on her doorstep every night. Eventually, people would talk. And she'd already had enough gossip surrounding her name to last a lifetime.

Her mind was made up. Caleb had to go. She just didn't know how to convince him to leave.

As promised, Caleb retrieved the cot from downstairs, along with a small pillow and thin blanket. As he set them up on the narrow landing in front of Tessa's front door, he glanced at the starlit sky. The moon was golden and round. No chance of a summer rainstorm tonight. The fragrant breeze blowing in from the east felt quite pleasant. The twinkling streetlights along Main Street offered a restful view of the town. All seemed right in the world. And yet, it was a facade.

As he lay down on the cot, he noticed his feet extended off the end. He didn't mind sleeping out in the open like this. A barrage of pleasurable recollections filled his mind. Hunting and fishing trips with his father and elder brothers. They always camped out beneath the stars at least once every summer. The venison and trout they acquired became part of their food storage. Caleb had always hoped to one day take his own wife and children on such outings. But those dreams had been dashed. Now, he had no wife and kids to build lovely memories with. Likewise, Sam had no father to take him on such excursions.

Caleb punched the lumpy pillow with his fist, then lay on his back and folded his arms behind his head. Gazing upward, he contemplated asking Tessa if she'd mind letting him take Sam on a short outing in the early autumn. Not too hot, but not too cold. Maybe Doris and Tessa would like to go as well. A little vacation might do them all some good. Getting away from the constant work would provide a nice break. He could hire Wilbur and Esther Schwartz to tend the diner for a handful of days while they were gone. The elderly couple were retired empty nesters. They didn't want to work regular hours, but they'd once owned a restaurant and bakery in Ronks, Pennsylvania, and were willing to fill in for a week or so if Caleb and his mom needed to leave town for a while.

A childless man and a fatherless boy. That was what

Caleb and Sam were. Maybe they needed each other. Maybe Tessa needed him, too…

His thoughts turned to what she'd said before stopping short. What had she meant about being brutalized? He wished she'd confide in him. When he'd pressed her for an explanation, she'd brushed him off. It was obvious she didn't want to talk about it. But something in her quivery voice, and the shattered look in her eyes, told him it had been traumatic. And once again, he wondered about Sam's father. What really happened five years ago when Tessa went to Denver on her *rumspringa*? What wasn't she telling him?

Sensing she needed more time to trust and confide in him, he didn't want to push her to talk about it. But for the first time since her return, his frozen heart softened a bit. Maybe he'd judged her too harshly. Against his better judgment, he sensed she needed his understanding. His compassion.

She was right to be worried about Bryce Jackson. For some reason, Tessa had become his target.

Caleb didn't want to provoke Bryce, nor did he want to pick a fight with the guy. Caleb would never use violence, but neither would he stand by and let Bryce hurt or terrorize Tessa and her young son. He'd heard the fear in Sam's voice when the boy had asked his mom if the bad man had returned. Sam was afraid of Bryce. Tessa couldn't even sleep at night. Enough was enough! Bryce Jackson had to quit coming around here and bothering Tessa. But how could they get the man to stop?

If Caleb had to sleep out beneath the stars every single night for the rest of his life, that was what he would do. With a little faith, Caleb would put his trust in *Gott*. Somehow, he'd keep Tessa and her sweet little son safe. And maybe someday, Tessa would set aside her reservations and finally tell him the truth.

Chapter Eleven

Tessa jerked awake and held perfectly still. She stared through the dark at the clock on the wall—2:38 in the morning. Her gritty eyes were filled with fatigue and she blinked, gazing up at the ceiling as she listened intently. Wondering what had awakened her.

Since her bedroom was two stories up, she felt safe to open her and Sam's windows. Muffled voices reached her ears, carried by the warm summer breeze. Sometimes, the heat made it difficult to sleep, and the gentle wind helped cool off the apartment.

The two voices sounded again. Two men, arguing about something. One seemed calm and reasoning, while the other was rather loud and angry.

She sat up and looked toward her open bedroom door. Were the men down in the alleyway? Or standing on the landing just outside her front door? She couldn't tell.

Throwing back the bedcovers, she swung her legs over the side of the mattress and reached for her modest bathrobe. After shrugging it on, she slid her feet into her slippers and shuffled across the hall to see that Sam was sleeping soundly. She quietly pulled his door closed. Twisting her long hair into a knot and letting it slide down her back inside her robe, she hurried to the living room. There wasn't time to pull her unbound hair into a bun and tuck it beneath her prayer *kapp*, but she could do her best to hide it from view.

The voices came again, right outside her front door. She heard the unmistakable soothing tones of Caleb's voice, then the thunderous, indignant yells of Bryce Jackson.

Oh, no! He was back. And since Caleb had been sleeping on her doorstep every night for the past three days, the two men were now embroiled in a conflict, and she didn't like it.

She pressed her cheek against the solid panel of her front door, trying to make out their words.

"You should go home, Bryce. It's late and you shouldn't be here," Caleb said.

"Well, what are you doing here?" Bryce asked, his comment slightly slurred.

"I'm looking out for Tessa and Sam because you keep harassing them. Leave now and don't come back here again," Caleb said, his tone still completely unruffled but filled with an insistent edge of determination.

"Oh, yeah? And who put you in charge of her? You're not the boss of me, either. It's a free world and I can do what I want," Bryce yelled at the top of his voice.

"Not if it means you're terrifying Tessa and Sam. Think about the little boy and how you're frightening him," Caleb said, his tone now carrying a deadly edge of fury.

Tessa wondered if Caleb might strike Bryce. Would he resort to violence in order to defend her? She couldn't allow that to happen.

"Yeah? And what are you gonna do about it?" Bryce asked, his voice filled with belligerence.

There was a short pause, and Tessa could just imagine the two men standing nose to nose on the narrow landing, glaring into one another's eyes.

"If you don't stay away, I'll have no choice but to report you to the sheriff," Caleb said.

The sheriff! Tessa couldn't believe it. Had it come to that?

A low growl sounded, and Tessa thought it came from Bryce.

"You can't tell me what to do," Bryce said.

"I mean it. You leave and don't come back. Right now," Caleb said, an edge of rage lacing his words.

"Why, you…" came Bryce's reply.

A hard thump struck the outside of the door, as if a fist or body had fallen against it. Tessa gasped and jerked away, thinking they must be fighting. Though Caleb had done an admirable job of maintaining his temper, Tessa could tell he was getting angry. And what if he lost control and struck Bryce? That could have disastrous consequences. Caleb could be shunned by everyone in their congregation. All the Amish who frequented the diner would no longer give Caleb their business. They could not speak to him nor accept anything from his hand.

And even worse, if Caleb reported Bryce to the

Englisch sheriff, it could destroy Caleb's diner. Bryce was related by blood to half the *Englisch* people in this town. They all knew he was a drunkard, but they wouldn't like it if Caleb got him in trouble with the law. In fact, the *Englischers* might stop coming to the diner, too. And Caleb needed their patronage to survive. Without the business from the diner, Caleb and Doris would lose their livelihood. And Tessa would lose her job.

Surely, Caleb knew this situation could destroy his living. And yet, here he was, sleeping on her doorstep, trying to fend off Bryce. Defending her and Sam.

Tessa couldn't sit by and do nothing while Caleb's livelihood was destroyed. She would not stand for it.

At that moment, something boiled up inside her. Something she'd never felt before in her entire life. A righteous indignation that filled her with such powerful outrage that she flipped the dead bolt and threw open the door and stepped out onto the landing to confront Bryce Jackson.

"What do you think you're doing?" she said, using her outraged mother's voice as she placed her hands on her hips.

The two men stared in surprise. She could tell that she'd taken them off-guard and they hadn't expected her to come outside.

In a glance, Tessa could see Caleb's cot had been overturned, the pillow and blanket lying on the wooden landing. Caleb stood against the wall, obviously backed into a corner by Bryce. But even with only the street-lights and moonlight to clarify her view, she could see that Caleb's face was red and filled with anger, his fists tight at his sides. She had only minutes to defuse this situation before he lost his temper and hit the other man.

She faced Bryce and took a step toward him.

"What do you want?" she asked, her tone filled with censure and a lot of indignation.

He blinked and backed up a step. "I... I just wanted to see you, was all."

She took a deep breath and narrowed her eyes. Her entire body pulsed with righteous outrage. "Bryce Jackson, do you realize what time it is?"

"Um, no, I don't." Bryce glanced at his left wrist, but he wasn't wearing a watch.

"It is late, and nothing *gut* happens after midnight. If you want to speak with me, you can do so in the diner during regular operating hours. But I will expect you to act like a gentleman then. Right now, I have a little boy inside and we are trying to sleep. You have no right to come pounding on my door in the middle of the night. I want you to go away and never return to my home again. Do you understand me, sir?"

His mouth dropped open, and he just stared at her. "I... I, yes, ma'am. I understand."

"*Gut!* Then, you turn around right now and walk down those stairs and go home. You should be asleep, too." She pointed to add emphasis.

He glanced at Caleb, who now stood beside her. His hands were raised slightly, as if he was prepared to push Bryce away if the man decided to attack Tessa.

"I... I'm sorry." Bryce backed up, stumbled against the top step and flailed for a moment before he gripped the handrail. He was obviously inebriated. "I didn't mean to upset you. I… I'm really sorry, Tessa. I didn't mean to bother you. I won't bother you again."

He turned and headed down the stairs. Midway, he missed a step, lost his balance and fell head over teakettle the rest of the way to the ground.

Tessa gasped and would have rushed down the stairs to render aid, but Caleb shot out an arm and held her back.

"Leave him. Let him get up on his own. It'll emphasize the lesson you just taught him," Caleb murmured softly.

Tessa wasn't so sure. She pushed against Caleb, but he took hold of her shoulders and held her tight. Together, they watched as Bryce groaned and pushed himself up. She stared at the man as he stumbled off into the night, yelling some obscene phrases that caused Tessa to cover her ears in outrage.

Watching him go, she felt her pulse settle to a normal rate, and her heart stopped pounding wildly. But something had changed inside her. Something she didn't fully understand. Bryce had intimidated her several times now, but this time was different. He'd threatened not only her sleeping son, but Caleb and his livelihood, too. And she was not going to see that happen. No, not if she could do something about it. Because she was determined never to be hurt, brutalized or used by any man again.

Caleb gazed at Tessa's profile as she watched Bryce Jackson stumble away. Caleb stood there several moments, letting his hands relax slightly as they gripped her upper arms. The beauty of her gleaming face helped settle his nerves. Several silken strands of her long, blond hair had come free of her bathrobe and cascaded down to her hip. Because they always kept it hidden beneath their prayer *kapps*, he'd rarely seen an Amish woman's long hair. It was a prize they kept for their husband's view only. And looking at Tessa, he again thought he'd never seen such a beautiful woman in all his life.

"Do you…do you think he's *allrecht*?" Tessa asked. "Maybe we should go after him, to ensure he's okay."

Caleb almost laughed. Bryce Jackson had been terrorizing Tessa, and yet she was worried about the man's welfare. And that was when Caleb realized she hadn't changed so much over the past few years. She was still spunky, but she was also kind, gentle and caring toward others.

"*Ne*, he's fine," Caleb said.

She turned her face to look up at him. Meeting his eyes, her voice was a soft whisper. "But what if he's hurt? After all, he has become a slave to strong drink. Even though he's our *feind*, we are beholden to help him, if we can."

Caleb's breath stilled in his throat. Bryce was their enemy? He didn't think of him that way. All Caleb could do was pity the man. Bryce was a drunkard with a nasty temper, and his life was in ruins. But still, Tessa was right. No matter what, the Lord wanted them to befriend even their adversaries. To show an increase of love toward those who would spitefully use them. They should always turn the other cheek. But in this situation, Caleb had no doubt Bryce was all right. It would be best for him to go home and lick his wounds and think about what Tessa had said. Maybe her words would make a great difference in Bryce's future actions.

"He will go *heemet* now and sleep it off. And in the morning, he might make some changes in his life. That's all we can hope for," Caleb said.

"But what if he returns?" she asked, her gentle breath brushing against his chin.

"I don't believe he will come back. Not after the scolding you just gave him."

He smiled, appreciating her righteous outrage as she'd told off Bryce Jackson. Never in his life had Caleb seen Tessa react with such strength and force. She'd been absolutely splendid in the power of her scorn. And yet, she hadn't lifted a finger in defense of herself.

"You were magnificent," Caleb said, meaning every word.

She tilted her head to the side, her eyes filled with questions. "I don't understand."

"The way you told off Bryce Jackson," he said. "You never raised your voice or lifted a hand to him. And yet, with your words and demeanor alone, you overpowered and humbled him, sending him running off into the night with his tail tucked between his legs."

She snorted and gave him a slight smile of satisfaction. "I did kind of tell him off, didn't I?"

He nodded, mesmerized by her smile. "You did more than that, Tessie. You frightened me, too. You're not a woman to mess with. I doubt he'll ever return."

She met his eyes again, a slight frown crinkling her forehead. "I frightened you?"

He nodded again as he lowered his face just a bit. "You did. I'm glad Sam is such a well-behaved child. I'd hate to have your mom's voice used on me."

She gave a little laugh and curled into his arms, drawing slightly nearer. He felt lost in her beautiful blue eyes. A melty feeling seized his heart, and he was transfixed by her gentle gaze. For years, he'd loved this woman. He'd thought of nothing but working to build a life with her by his side. And then she'd dashed his dreams by going to Denver without him. She'd shattered his world. Now, here she was. Warm and soft and wrapped within his arms.

Could he trust her now? He wasn't sure. But as he held her, that didn't seem to matter. Not at that moment.

He kissed her, and she responded, lifting the palms of her hands to cover his chest. A soft caress that caused him to close his eyes and pretend for just a few seconds that she was his again and they'd never been hurt, never lost their love. Then she pushed him away.

"*Ne*, Caleb. We can't," she said, stepping back toward the door.

He released her, letting her go. Staring at her as feelings of shock and wonder overwhelmed him at the same time.

"Why, Tessie? Why can't you tell me what happened to us so we can put aside the past and start anew? That's what I want. To make a fresh start," he said.

She shook her head and reached for the doorknob. Turning it, she stepped inside before looking back at him. "I can't, Caleb. Too much has happened for me to forget. You deserve a better woman than I can ever be. Please! Please let me go and pretend this night never happened."

As she closed the door between them, his heart gave a hard thump of regret. He heard the dead bolt slide into place, and still he stood there, staring at the portal.

Never had he felt so frustrated in all his life. How he wished Tessa would talk to him. How he wished they could forget the past and move forward into a loving future. He was willing, but something held her back. Something traumatic and horrible. He knew it instinctively, without her telling him. And that was when an idea occurred to him. She was frightened of men. He'd seen it clearly every time Bryce Jackson got near her. And just now, when he'd touched her, she'd let her guard down for a moment, but soon put the walls back up.

There were times in the restaurant when she'd responded toward Caleb with fear. That never happened before she went to Denver. When they'd been going to school together, she'd always been so affectionate and loving. So open and secure in her relationships. So, what had happened to make her change?

Only one thing came to mind, and just thinking about it caused his heart to squeeze painfully in his chest.

He set the cot aright and placed the pillow and blanket atop the thin mattress before lying down again. He doubted Bryce Jackson would return, but it was too late at night for him to go home. He'd warned his mom that he might stay at the diner all night. Doris knew Bryce had been hassling Tessa and didn't ask questions. Yet, he couldn't sleep. His mind churned with riotous thoughts that caused him to wince with anguish.

Someone had hurt Tessa. He knew it deep inside the core of his being. A part of him said it was her own fault. She'd gone to Denver when he'd warned her not to go. She was sweet, hardworking and feisty. Much too worldly. She had put herself in a bad situation she couldn't control. But another part of him said she didn't deserve what had happened to her. No one did. She'd suffered enough for her actions. It was time to forgive and forget. He knew that deep in his heart.

Someone had brutalized her, and that made him angry. He reminded himself that *Gott* wouldn't approve of such emotions. Nor would Tessa.

He owned the diner and was her boss. He couldn't fire her. Not when she was doing such a good job and seemed so desperate to retain her independence. But working with her, being near her, smelling the warm, sweet fragrance of her skin, was getting more and more difficult every day. He'd always known it wasn't a good idea to hire her. Now, the three-month deadline they'd agreed upon was fast approaching. How could he continue like this once it arrived?

He couldn't. And that put them both in a highly precarious position.

Something would have to change. And soon. But he didn't know what. He couldn't move forward, yet they couldn't go back, either. Because she didn't love him anymore. And that hurt most of all.

Chapter Twelve

A week later, Tessa was working in the diner when they ran out of salad mix. They'd had a huge lunch rush, but the foot traffic seemed to die down by midafternoon. Having bussed most of the tables, she'd wheeled the heavy tubs into the farthest back room and was loading dirty dishes into the industrial-size dishwasher when Caleb startled her.

"Tessa?"

She jerked, glanced at him, then focused on the sudsy water as she scrubbed an oversize stock pot. After the kiss they'd shared, she still couldn't bring herself to meet his eyes.

"I need to run over to the grocery store and buy some more lettuce to last us until our delivery truck arrives in the morning. Is there anything else we need?" he asked.

He was the owner, yet it seemed they'd become a team as they worked together in the diner. She knew he'd come to rely on her. And heaven help her, she'd become much too dependent on him.

"*Ja*, we're low on cherry tomatoes, too," she said.

Not a critical issue. They could just leave the tomatoes out of the salad bar.

"Got it. And you'll be *allrecht* while I'm gone?" he asked.

His consideration surprised her, and she felt the undercurrent of his concern. He wasn't just asking if she could hold down the fort. He was also asking if she could deal with Bryce Jackson if he came into the restaurant again.

As Caleb had predicted, Bryce hadn't returned to her apartment. He'd been in the diner for breakfast just that morning with two of his cronies, but he'd barely looked her way. She'd refused to hide in the kitchen, remaining in the dining room instead. Never again would she cower before any man. And when she'd taken Bryce's order, he'd sat still as stone and barely looked at her. In fact, he'd seemed almost afraid of her, if that was possible. But she'd noticed one huge change—he seemed sober for the first time since she'd met him, and he wore a clean shirt and had shaved and combed his hair, too. The shift in his personal hygiene was startling, and she wondered if perhaps Caleb was right. Maybe standing up to him had made a difference after all.

"*Ja*, I can manage just fine," she said, remembering the tender kiss they'd shared several nights earlier.

They hadn't discussed what had happened, but she was highly aware of him, and a rush of heat seared her cheeks. Somehow, that kiss had changed things, reminding her that the physical attraction was still there between them, bigger than life. But she mustn't encourage him. Not when he'd declared he'd like to make a fresh start with her. In that moment, she'd realized he'd forgiven her for breaking his heart. But the problem went much deeper than that...

Because she couldn't forgive herself.

"We'll be fine while you're gone. You go ahead," she murmured, still not looking at him.

He stepped away, and she felt the vibrations of his footsteps as he retreated. She caught the low thrum of Doris's voice in the kitchen as she bade him farewell, then heard the back screen door as it clapped closed behind him. The general store was only two blocks away. He wouldn't be gone long.

A few minutes later, she heard the clatter of stainless steel clanking together and wondered what Doris was up to. She knew the woman would alert her if a new customer came into the restaurant.

After rinsing the large pot, Tessa picked up a dish towel and dried it before setting it aside. She'd just pulled the plug and let the soapy water drain from the sink when Sam ran into the washroom.

"*Mammi!* Come quick. Something's wrong with Doris," the boy cried as he tugged on her apron.

Tossing the towel aside, Tessa hurried after the boy as he raced back into the kitchen. Doris was slumped against the counter, gasping and clutching her chest, her face contorted with pain. A variety of long-handled stainless-steel spoons and utensils lay around her, as if she'd dropped them.

"Doris! Are you *allrecht*?" Tessa cried.

There were no chairs in the room, so she helped the woman slide down to sit on the floor. Sam stood nearby, his eyes and forehead creased like he was about to cry.

If only Caleb was here, he'd know exactly what to do. But she was on her own, and Doris's life depended on her quick actions.

"Is it your heart?" Tessa asked.

Unable to speak coherently, Doris nodded.

"Where are your nitroglycerin pills?" Though Tessa had never witnessed a heart attack before, she'd heard enough to know the woman had a prescription from her doctor.

Doris glanced toward the office.

"I'll get them," Tessa said, noticing the woman's skin was clammy to the touch and pale as fresh cream.

She bolted to her feet and raced off, pawing around the desk until she found Doris's purse. Tessa's hands were shaking like a leaf, so she dumped the bag upside down on the top of the desk. The bottle of pills fell out with the other contents. Snapping it up, she hurried back to the kitchen and helped Doris take one.

"Just breathe deep," Tessa encouraged as she rubbed the woman's back in a soothing gesture.

A few scant minutes later, Doris was breathing easy enough to speak.

"The pain...it's still here," Doris gasped, clutching folds of her dress across her chest.

"I'll get help," Tessa said. She glanced at her son as she headed toward the dining room. "Stay with Doris, Sam. Don't go anywhere until I return."

He nodded, his eyes wide and solemn.

There was a telephone in the back office for food orders and emergencies, but Caleb always took the calls. Tessa had no idea how to use the phone. And she didn't want to waste precious time trying to figure it out. After her experience with Bryce Jackson, she realized she couldn't do everything on her own. She needed to ask others for assistance. Right now. Before it was too late.

"Please help me," she called as she ran into the dining room.

Five *Englisch* customers sat at two tables, three men together and two teenaged girls. They all turned to look at her, their faces filled with surprise.

"We have an emergency. Can someone call for an ambulance right away?" Tessa asked, her voice breathless and anxious.

The men each reached toward their pants pockets, but one of the girls was faster, poking in the numbers before anyone else could react.

"What's happened? What's wrong?" Bart Sullivan asked, rising from his seat.

A tall, older man with kind brown eyes and a short gray beard, Bart usually wore khaki slacks and a colorful polo shirt to the diner. He wasn't a rancher. Tessa had overheard that he'd come to Riverton from Kansas, but had no idea what he'd done for a living there.

The burn of tears filled her eyes, and she blinked them away. "It's Doris. She has a bad heart. I think she's having a heart attack."

"I'm a retired doctor. Let's take a look," he said.

Oh, those words were sweet to Tessa's ears.

She led the way, racing back to the kitchen with Bart hot on her heels. She stood aside as the doctor knelt over the woman. Tessa felt Sam sidle up against her and slip his hand into hers. One of the teenaged girls stood in the doorway, and Tessa had the presence of mind to have her take Sam out into the dining room to wait. If Doris died, she didn't want him to witness the scene.

"Doris, are you having chest pains?" Bart asked, checking her eyes and pulse.

Doris nodded.

"Did you pass out?" he asked.

She shook her head.

"She just took her medication a few minutes ago," Tessa supplied.

"Good," Bart said.

While checking her pulse again, he asked Doris a few more questions.

Soon, they heard the thin wail of a siren pulling up outside. Within moments, two young men wearing dark uniforms entered the kitchen.

Tessa stood back as the medics asked almost verbatim the same questions Bart had directed at Doris. One man took her blood pressure while the other covered her mouth and nose with an oxygen mask. Within minutes, they had placed her on a gurney and strapped her down so she wouldn't fall off. They were just wheeling her out of the diner when Caleb returned. Though it seemed like he'd been gone for hours, Tessa realized it had been no more than twenty minutes.

"I heard the siren. What's going on?" Caleb asked, his face filled with fear as he looked at his mother.

"It appears Doris had another heart attack. I gave her a pill, and Bart is a retired doctor. I had one of the customers call an ambulance. I hope that's *allrecht*," Tessa said.

Caleb hurried toward the front door with the medics, speaking urgently over his shoulder. "Of course it's okay. I've got to go with her. Can you close up the diner for me?"

Of course she could. She did so almost every night. But the fact that he asked her seemed so unassuming. And considering the situation was quite serious, yet he still was thoughtful of her, she liked that about him. Again, his trust in her brought a warm feeling to her heart.

"*Ja*, I'll take care of everything. I'll take care of your horse, too. You just go," Tessa called back.

And just like that, he was gone. Standing in front of the wide picture windows, Tessa watched with the other customers as the men loaded Doris into the ambulance. Caleb hopped inside before Bart slammed the double doors closed and the vehicle pulled away.

Since they only had one small hospital in town, Tessa knew exactly where they were going. But one thought pounded her brain. What if Doris died? Was this the last time she'd ever see the sweet Amish woman alive? Since Tessa had returned from Denver, Doris had been one of her only true friends, and she loved her like a mother. Tessa couldn't stand to lose the woman. Not now. Not like this.

"Tessa, what can I do to help?"

She turned and found a heavily pregnant Lovina Lapp standing beside her. Like many of the Amish, she frequented the diner, and Tessa considered her a friend. She had no idea when Lovina had come into the restaurant, but she was glad to see a smiling face.

Her mind raced. "I... I need to close the diner and get to the hospital. If anything happens to Doris, I..."

She didn't finish the sentence. The tenets of her faith dictated that she must accept *Gott*'s will in all things. She must have the courage to face whatever came her way. Caleb would be beside himself with grief if he lost Doris. He loved his mother dearly, and none of his siblings lived nearby. He was alone, like Tessa. She needed to be there to comfort him, just in case.

"*Mammi*, is Doris gonna die?" Sam asked, exhaling a shuddering breath before wiping his dripping nose on the sleeve of his shirt.

Tessa picked up her son and cuddled him close as she wiped his tearstained face with a corner of her apron. It would do him no good for her to lie. She couldn't shield him from the facts. Though the Amish suffered grief like anyone else, death was a part of life, and they were determined to trust in *Gott*.

"I don't know, *sohn*," she said. "We must pray and have faith. Doris is in the Lord's hands now. Caleb is with her, and I know they'll do everything they can for her at the hospital."

The stress and anguish must have shown on her face, because Lovina wrapped an arm around her shoulders and gave her a tight squeeze. It felt good to have a friend there to offer support.

"I'll tell you what," Lovina said. "Why don't I take Sam *heemet* with me, and I'll pour him a nice cool glass of lemonade to go with some fresh chocolate chip cookies I made this morning?"

Sam immediately nodded, and Lovina reached to take him from Tessa, holding him on her hip.

"You can help me tend Autumn while your *mamm* goes to the hospital," Lovina continued.

Tessa glanced at Lovina's distended tummy, then met the woman's eyes. The woman was eight months pregnant and had a young daughter at home. Tessa didn't want to do anything to cause an early birth.

"*Ach*, are you sure you feel up to watching Sam?" Tessa asked.

"Of course. Jonah will be there to help. I'll send him over to Caleb's place to feed and water his livestock so you won't need to worry about that tonight. It's a pleasure to serve," she said.

Tessa wasn't worried about Caleb's farm. She knew word would soon spread among their Amish people that Doris was in the hospital. By tomorrow morning, a flock of men and women would descend on Caleb's farm and perform every chore on the place. It was the Amish way, to take care of one another in times of need. Doris, Caleb and Tessa had done it for other people in the past. Now, it was their turn to be on the receiving end. And it was a tremendous blessing Tessa never took for granted.

"If it gets too late in the evening, I'll give Sam his supper and put him to bed with my Autumn. He'll be my big helper today, won't you, Sam?" Lovina smiled at the boy, then looked at Tessa again. "You can *komm* and pick him up in the morning. If he needs to stay with me for a few days, that's fine, too. As long as you need. You've got your hands full here, helping Caleb with the diner."

"*Danke*. I so appreciate it," Tessa said, feeling over whelmed by Lovina's kindness

"But I wanna go see Doris," Sam said, his voice quavering.

Tessa knew her son was upset. He loved Doris, too. It helped that Lovina wasn't a stranger to him. The boy knew her well, and he'd been over to her house numerous times. The Amish were a tight-knit group. Though Tessa hadn't felt like she fully belonged, she realized now that was a discrepancy within her own mind and not because she hadn't been accepted by her people. And for the first time since she'd returned from Denver, she reconsidered her position within this community. Maybe she had more friends here than she realized. Maybe she belonged after all.

"I know you want to see Doris, *liebchen*, but she's very sick and I doubt the *dokder* will let her have visitors right now," she said. "We're trying to do everything we can to make sure she gets better. I love you and I'll *komm* to Lovina's house for you as soon as I can. *Allrecht?*" she said.

He frowned, looking doubtful. But at least his tears had stopped. *"Allrecht."*

She kissed his cheek and watched as Lovina smiled and carried him out the door. With her little boy taken care of, Tessa was able to focus on the diner. She quickly cleared the place of customers, touched by their expressions of concern and support, even though they were *Englisch* and she was Amish. Then, she wrote a large sign and taped it to the front window to explain they were closed due to an emergency. After locking the door and lowering the blinds, she hurried into the kitchen and ensured the grill and stove were turned off and all the food was properly put away.

Then she stepped out into the alley and locked the back door behind her.

Hurrying over to Caleb's road horse, she stepped up into the buggy, took the leather lead lines in a practiced grip and hurried off to the hospital. As she drove down Main Street, she let the rhythmic clip-clop of the animal's hooves settle her nerves. And in the quiet moments that followed, she whispered a silent prayer, asking *Gott* to help Doris recover and provide her, Sam and Caleb the courage to accept His will.

Caleb sat in the waiting room of the hospital, anxious to hear news about his mother. Leaning forward, he rested his elbows on his knees and fisted his hands together as he stared at the wall. The smell of bitter antiseptic hung in the air. A persistent beep down the hall caused him to close his eyes. By all outward appearances, he seemed completely calm. But inside, he was screaming. The last time *Mamm* had a heart attack, the doctor had warned the next one could be fatal. And Caleb wasn't prepared to lose his mother. Not now. Not when she was still so young. She was someone he confided in. His dearest friend.

No, there was another. But he couldn't think about Tessa right now. Not when his mother might be dying. Though he cared deeply for her and considered her a cherished friend, she didn't feel the same toward him. In fact, if not for her employment at his diner, she'd have nothing to do with him. But somehow, over the past few months, things had changed. He'd watched her closely, looking for any sign of the flighty, worldly girl she'd once been. But all he saw was a fully matured woman of faith with a diligent work ethic and unconditional love for her child. And Caleb couldn't help admiring Tessa.

A subtle sound came from the doorway. He looked up, and there she was. Tessa. The girl of his dreams.

She walked toward him and he stood, meeting her halfway. In spite of feeling overpowered by fear, a thrill of excitement shot through him. Until that moment, he hadn't realized how much he yearned to see her. To confide in her. To tell her how frightened he was. To beg her to give their relationship a second chance.

"Tessa."

He said her name on a sigh, wishing he could fold her into his arms and weep against her shoulder. But strong men didn't cry. His father had taught him that years ago. It just wasn't done. Not among the Amish. Showing overly strong emotions such as fear and grief indicated a lack of trust in *Gott*. And right now, Caleb knew his faith was all he had. So, he clung to it with all his might. Hoping. Praying. Desperate for his mother to be okay and for Tessa to finally accept him. At least, that was the prayer he sent upward to heaven.

She smiled and touched his arm with her fingertips, speaking in that soft, mesmerizing voice of hers. "Has there been any news yet?"

He shook his head. "*Ne*, I haven't spoken with the doctor. The nurse said they were doing an electrocardiogram and are running some other tests."

There was a long pause as they sat together, each of them lost in their own thoughts.

"Where's Sam? Were you able to close up the diner and take care of Tommy okay?" he asked.

"*Ja*, Lovina Lapp is watching Sam for me, and Jonah is going to feed and water your livestock this evening. I've got your horse outside in the parking lot. When I leave, I'll take him to your farm and see that he's well tended."

He glanced toward the doorway, feeling edgy and impatient for some news. "What could be taking so long?"

Tessa shrugged and rested her hand on his. Her touch was soft, warm and wonderful. "Tests take time. We've got to have faith that she'll be okay."

He met her eyes and felt a melting inside his heart. A feeling that what she said was true. His mother would recover, and all would be well. He hoped so.

"I did everything I could to lighten her load," he said. "I tried to get her to eat right and take her medication. I hired you so she could rest. But she just kept on working. Every time I turned around, she was busy doing some task. And when I got after her for it, she just laughed and said she could rest when she was dead."

He looked down, staring at their hands. Feeling the weight of the world on his shoulders.

Tessa sighed. "*Ja*, she always says that. But we have to remember it's difficult for people who have been active and vital all their lives to suddenly stop working. Doris confided to me that she'd rather be dead than useless."

He blinked at that, looking concerned. "She said that?"

Tessa nodded, showing a wan smile. "She didn't want to be a burden. And I can't blame her. I'd feel the same."

"She isn't a burden. Not at all. It's just that I'm so busy all the time," he said.

"Of course you are. You're earning a living, like everyone else. And she knows that. But sometimes, I think there are worse things than death. And Doris wants to stay busy. Maybe we could find her something to do that requires very little lifting or physical labor. Maybe she could crochet doilies and afghans to sell at the farmers market," she suggested.

The notion lit up his mind. "*Ach*, that's a *gut* idea. Why didn't I think of that?"

She chuckled. "Because you're a man, and men don't think about things like crochet."

He laughed, feeling better now she was here. "You're right about that. Us men need you women to teach us such things."

They were quiet again, with just the sounds of people talking out at the reception desk. Finally, he glanced at her and asked the question that had been grinding inside his mind for years now.

"Why hasn't Sam's *vadder* come to take him and you away? Who is the man, and why isn't he here with you now?" he asked.

Tessa withdrew her hand from his and looked away. She made a low, strangled sound in the back of her throat, and he knew he'd taken her off guard. Her shoulders stiffened, and she clenched her hands. For a moment, he thought she might get up and leave the room without any explanation. But he waited, giving her time to gather her thoughts. He'd been patient long enough and was dying to know the truth. It was time. He just hoped she believed that, too.

Finally, she opened her mouth and spoke in a hoarse whisper filled with pain and regret. She told him everything. How she'd gone to a party at a house filled with strangers and accepted a drink from a young *Englisch* man. She'd felt dizzy afterward and soon lost consciousness. Early the next morning, she'd awoken, her body bruised and violated. She'd left immediately and gotten on the first bus back to Riverton. And a few months later, she'd discovered she was expecting a baby.

She met his gaze, her eyes filled with tears that overflowed and raced down her cheeks. She wiped them away with the back of her hand. "Now you know why I've never told you or anyone what happened. I don't know a lot about Sam's *vadder*. Not really. Even if I wanted to, I have no idea how to find him. But I would never go in search of the man. He's *Englisch* and, after what he did to me, he can't be trusted. I don't want him in mine or Sam's lives. Not ever. And if word gets out, it could hurt my little *sohn*. I don't want him to feel different or ever believe he isn't loved. I want him to grow up knowing how much I adore him and want him in my life."

She stared at her hands, twined together in her lap. She looked so small and defenseless sitting beside him. So innocent and vulnerable. Then, she looked at him, and desperation filled her eyes.

"*Ach*, please don't tell anyone, Caleb. Not even Doris. If you do, word will get out. Sam will find out one day. Maybe not now, but later down the road, when he's older, someone will tell him. Something like this could be used as a weapon against him. Maybe one of his school mates might be thoughtless and angry and tell him out of spite. And I don't want him to feel bad about his birth. It wasn't his fault. He was innocent in what happened. He must never know the truth."

Caleb blinked, unable to deny the fierce pleading in her quiet voice. Now he knew. And yet, it changed none of his newly realized feelings for her. Instead, it made him feel ashamed.

"It's odd, but I feel relieved now that I've finally shared my secret with someone I trust," she said. She turned to him, her eyes damp, her face filled with a serenity he hadn't seen in her for years. "I've carried the burden alone for so long that it had become heavy and difficult for me. *Danke* for letting me confide in you. You've always been so kind to me, and I'll always cherish our friendship. But now, it's time for us both to move on with our lives. You need to date some of the eligible young women in our congregation. You must marry and raise a *familye* of your own."

He reached for her hand, but she pulled it away.

"*Ne*, Caleb. You must listen to me. It's finished between us. I have Sam to think about now. It's time for you to move on and find someone else."

What? He couldn't let it end like this. Not after everything she'd just told him. "Tessie, I…"

"Ahem! Excuse me, Mr. Yoder."

In unison, they looked toward the door and saw an older *Englisch* man wearing a white smock with a stethoscope dangling around his neck. They both came to their feet as the doctor walked toward them and held out a hand, which Caleb shook. Since there were only two doctors in this small town, Caleb knew the man well.

"Dr. McGann, how is she?" Caleb asked.

"She's awake and stable," Dr. McGann said.

Relief flooded Caleb's heart. "Is she going to be okay?"

"At the present, she is doing quite well. After her last heart attack, I feared the next one would be fatal. But I'm pleased to report it was a small heart attack and she seems to be doing fine, all things considered. I have to say your mother got off easy this time around," the doctor said.

Caleb shook his head. "It was *Gott*'s will."

The doctor showed a tolerant smile. "I have no doubt God has answered all of our prayers today."

Caleb hid his surprise. He knew many *Englisch* people believed in *Gott* and tried to follow the teachings of Jesus Christ, but to hear that the doctor had offered a prayer on behalf of Doris touched Caleb's heart.

"Danke," Caleb said.

The doctor nodded. "Doris will need more rest and a drastic change to her diet. She really needs to lose twenty pounds. I think she can do that if she eats more fresh fruits and vegetables and fewer fried foods. I've also got a different medication I want her to start taking for her high blood pressure. I'd like to keep her here for observation tonight and see how she's doing in the morning. At this rate, I think she should be able to go home in a day or two."

"That's wonderful," Tessa said.

"*Ja*, that is *gut* news," Caleb agreed, unable to hide his deep relief. "And we'll help her watch what she eats, won't we, Tessa? We can assist her in losing a little weight."

"We sure will." Tessa nodded, looking as pleased by this tremendous news as he was.

"You can see her now, if you'll follow me," Dr. McGann said.

The doctor led the way down a long hallway. Caleb followed, with Tessa trailing behind. The doctor stopped at a room and stood back, indicating they should go inside. Doris was sitting up in bed, an IV in her arm and wires hooked up to her chest. A monitor and other equipment sat nearby, making low beeps now and then.

"*Sohn!*" Doris exclaimed when she saw him.

He came forward and leaned over to kiss her cheek. She pulled him close and squeezed his shoulders with her free arm. When he stood straight, Tessa leaned over and kissed Doris, too.

"I'm so happy you're doing better. You had us awfully worried for a while," Tessa said.

"I was worried myself. If you hadn't been there, I don't know what I would have done," Doris said.

Tessa lifted a hand in the air. "I did nothing. It was all *Gott*'s will."

"Actually—" the doctor spoke from the foot of the bed "—if you hadn't administered Doris her medication and then called the ambulance when you did, we might not have had such a happy outcome. I have no doubt your quick actions are what saved your mother-in-law's life today."

"Oh, she…she's not my mother-in-law. We're not married." Tessa gestured toward Caleb.

The doctor just smiled and looked pleased with himself.

Caleb didn't say a word. He didn't know what to think. Tessa had saved his mother's life today. She'd worked at the diner and on his farm and been there for them when they needed her the most. But he hadn't been there for Tessa in Denver. She'd been brutalized because he hadn't put her wants and needs before his own.

Within minutes, Tessa made her excuses and left. Caleb longed to talk to her some more. To tell her how he really felt. But honestly, he didn't know. And with Doris and various medical staff coming and going, Caleb realized this wasn't the right time to discuss their future. He needed to sort out his feelings. For years, Tessa had let him believe she'd betrayed him. That she'd fallen in love and had a child with another man. Now, he was just finding out that wasn't so. But why hadn't she told him the truth sooner? Had their relationship been so shallow that she hadn't felt she could trust him? Or was it something worse? Maybe what happened to her had killed her love for him, too.

And how did he feel about her? He wasn't sure anymore. What she'd told him changed everything and nothing between them. For the past five years, she hadn't trusted him enough to confide the facts to him. And he'd been so angry at her. So hurt and resentful.

So, where did that leave them? Nowhere! Because

without trust and love, they could never be together as a couple. And right now, he had no idea how to change that.

Chapter Thirteen

Tessa rang open the cash register in the diner, counted out the change for the last customer of the day and laid it in their hand.

"Thank you," she said, returning their smile.

As they turned and exited the diner, the bell above the door tinkled. Sliding the till drawer closed, Tessa glanced at the clock on the wall. Ten minutes past closing time.

She hurried around the counter and locked the door, then flipped the Closed sign around. Next, she lowered the blinds to shut out the heat of the bright summer sun. Taking a deep breath, she let it go as she gazed at the expansive dining room. Other than the hum of the soft-serve ice cream machine, all was quiet and still. She made a mental note of the chores she still needed to complete: empty and clean out the coffee maker, bus two dirty tables, wash the dishes in the back, refill the ketchup and mustard bottles, empty the garbage cans, sanitize the bathrooms and mop the floors. It wouldn't take long, and then she'd ride with Caleb and Sam to the farm, where she'd gather eggs, feed the chickens and pigs, and skim the cream before going home. She didn't mind the work. It kept her thoughts off her relationship with Caleb.

He was in the kitchen, finishing his own responsibilities for the day. Doris was home resting. For the past two weeks, the women of their congregation had been popping in and out of the farm each day to take Doris her lunch and ensure she was doing okay. Their generosity made it so Caleb could keep working while also caring for his mom at night. Doris was now doing well. Beginning next week, she would be able to prepare her own lunch. She'd started knitting baby hats and booties to sell on consignment at one of the stores in town. That kept her busy and off her feet. And of course, Caleb still made dinner for them all each evening. But Tessa didn't want to foist her active little boy off on the woman anymore. Not in her condition.

Lovina Lapp had been tending Sam for her. In fact, the kind midwife would be here any minute now, dropping Sam off at the back door. Because Tessa had to be at the restaurant so early each morning, Lovina or her husband had been picking up Sam and dropping him off every day since Doris's heart attack. But the closer Lovina came to her due date, the more Tessa realized she'd soon need to find other suitable childcare for her son.

Dumping the used coffee filter in the garbage, Tessa cleaned the machine, then prepped it for the morning rush. As she completed her duties, she let her mind wander.

At church last Sunday, Grace, Tessa's sister-in-law, had said she could watch Sam. That would be ideal, since the boy could go to school once he was old enough and play with his cousins during the day. But Wayne's place was located six miles outside town... twelve miles round trip. Tessa would have to get her son up at three o'clock each morning to make the drive there. And without a horse and buggy, it would be impossible for her to drop the boy off and pick him up each day. If she asked, Tessa knew Caleb would let her borrow his rig. But that would put him in a bind, since he would then have to walk back and forth to the diner. Since he brought fresh eggs, milk and cream with him every morning, that would be difficult without a buggy. And if Doris had another emergency, he wouldn't be able to respond as quickly. So, for now, there seemed no easy solutions. But Tessa would figure something out.

Hurrying with her work, she cleared the two tables, then wrung out her washrag and wiped them down. She lifted the heavy tub of dirty dishes and carried it to the back, walking quickly through the kitchen as she went. Caleb stood in front of the open refrigerator with his notepad and pencil, no doubt taking inventory of fresh vegetables, eggs and cream.

For two weeks, she'd avoided him as much as possible. Not once had he mentioned her trip to Denver five years earlier. Since that day in the hospital when she'd finally confided in him, they hadn't discussed anything but Doris and their work at the diner. Tessa preferred it that way. Just now, she hoped to pass by unnoticed, but he called to her.

"Tessa, if you have a minute, I'd like to speak with you, please."

She hesitated, and a sick feeling settled in her stomach. "Let me put these dishes in the sink to soak and I'll be right back."

At his nod, she hurried off but stayed overlong in the washroom, wondering what he wanted. She never should have told him what happened to her in Denver. When he hadn't asked any more questions, she'd thought perhaps they could pretend she'd never told him the truth and let it drop. But now, something told her his waiting was over. She dreaded the thought of facing him again.

"Tessa?"

She whirled around, startled out of her musings. *"Ja?"*

He stood beside the dish drain and leaned his hip against the counter. "Can we talk now?"

She shrugged, looking away. "What about?"

Though they had electricity in the diner, they didn't have an automatic dishwasher, so she reached for a towel and kept herself busy drying dishes.

"I… I wanted to tell you how sorry I am about what happened to you in Denver. I should have gone with you. If I'd been there, I could have protected you. I could have kept you safe. You never would have been hurt. I hope you'll forgive me for failing you," he said.

No, no, no! She didn't want him to apologize. It wasn't his fault. It wasn't her fault, either. She knew that now. It was her attacker's fault. Glen. It was his shame, not hers. But now, she had to live with the consequences. And it changed nothing between her and Caleb.

She turned aside, placing a stack of clean plates in the rack for quick removal in the morning. Her hands trembled.

"There is nothing to forgive. It wasn't your responsibility. It was mine. I put myself in a bad situation I couldn't control," she said, forcing herself not to meet his eyes. If she did, she feared she'd burst into tears.

"I appreciate your kind words," she continued, her voice sounding wobbly and nervous. "But you couldn't go with me. Your *vadder* needed you here at the diner. He wasn't feeling well, remember? I was foolish and impatient and wanted to go right then. I wasn't willing to wait for you. It was my fault for going, not yours."

He stepped near and laid a hand on her arm. His fingers felt warm, gentle and firm. She turned her head away, surprised by the sudden rush of tears. How she wished he would forget she'd ever told him.

"Tessie, please stop working for a moment. Can't you look at me?" he asked.

His voice was soft and cajoling. With his hand holding on to her, she had little choice but to look at him. She stood perfectly still and stared at the hollow of his throat.

"There's nothing to talk about. I'd rather let the subject drop. Please forget what I told you," she said.

He slid a strong hand behind her back and pulled her closer. "I can't forget. Not ever. I've had a lot of time to think about what you said. For a long time, I didn't understand why you pushed me away. I thought I'd done something wrong to make you stop loving me.

I was angry and hurt. Now, I understand how injured you were, too."

"You did nothing wrong," she cried.

"You did nothing wrong, either. You simply went to a party with friends. You should have been secure there. You had every right to be safe. But someone drugged you and took advantage. It wasn't your fault, either. Not at all. And I'm sorry I judged you so harshly," he said.

Oh, how she longed to believe what he said. Yes, she knew what he said was true. And yet, she couldn't forget about the anger, doubt and pain and pretend it had never happened. But it had. And she could never change the truth.

"Please don't tell anyone, Caleb. If people found out… I couldn't stand that," she said.

He showed a gentle smile. "I understand. Your secret is safe with me. I'll never tell another living soul. But I'd like us to be more than friends, Tessie. Can't we start anew? What happened to you makes no difference to me. I love you and Sam. I'd like us to be a *familye*," he said.

She went very still, yearning to give in to the enticing gentleness of his voice. To curl against his firm chest and let him love her as she had always loved him. For five long years, she'd been tortured by the knowledge that she'd broken his heart. That she was culpable for their breakup. She'd been too worldly and had run off to Denver against his wishes. And when she'd returned, she'd known how she'd hurt him and ruined her own life. The cruelest punishment of all was that she'd never stopped loving him. Not for one single moment. But he had to be doing this out of pity. Because he felt sorry for her. And she'd never marry a man for that reason.

Maybe she shouldn't have told him the truth. Now that he knew, he expected her to return to him. To forget what had happened. And she couldn't. She felt more ashamed than ever before. It had been unwise to confide in him. Because now he felt sorry for her. She loved him dearly, but she didn't want him to feel obligated to marry her. He was so good, so kind and dutiful. It wasn't his fault. He'd been a devoted son and remained behind in Riverton because his father needed him. If only Tessa had done the same. It had been a foolish notion to leave. But she had, and it had set their lives on a path she'd never expected. And yet, if she hadn't gone, she never would have become Sam's mommy. And in spite of everything that had happened, she couldn't regret her son. Not ever!

So, where did that leave them? What could she say or do to make Caleb leave her alone? How could she push him away?

She pressed a hand against his chest and stepped back. Locking her jaw, she glared at him with as much contempt as she could muster. Not an easy thing to do, considering he was the love of her life. But telling him the truth hadn't changed anything between them. He deserved a better woman than she could ever be. And if that meant she had to quit her job and move back in with Wayne and Grace, then so be it. She'd be beholden to her brother for the rest of her life. An unwanted burden, foisted on his *familye*. But she'd do it for Sam. Because he deserved to be safe and happy.

Because she was never going to marry Caleb as long as she believed he was doing it out of pity.

"We were finished long ago, Caleb. It could never work between us now," she said.

"It could if you'd let it. I'd like us to try," he said.

"*Ne*, I don't want you or any man to control my life. I want to make my own decisions and maintain as much freedom as possible for as long as I can." Her words were true, if taken out of context.

He smiled. "I've always admired your autonomy and initiative, Tessie. Maybe it wouldn't work for another Amish couple, but it can for us. I don't see a problem here. I see you as part of my team, not someone I can dominate."

"You say that now, but you would come to resent me later on. Maybe not at first, but one day, you wouldn't like me anymore," she said, wishing he wouldn't stand so close.

"Then we'd discuss things fairly. We'd work it out between the two of us. We'd come to an agreement on every important issue. And if not, then it must not be so important after all and I'd let it drop," he said.

"*Ne*, not if it's something serious that we disagreed on. Because you would be the man of the house, I'd be obligated to do whatever you want. But it's more than that. I won't marry a man who pities me," she said.

There. She'd finally said it out loud. The real crux of the problem.

"I love you. We would make it work, together. You and me. With compromise and respect for each other."

He stepped closer and lowered his head. Their gazes clashed, then locked. She couldn't look away to save her life. He loved her? She didn't believe it. He felt sorry for her, that was all.

"*Ne*, Caleb," she said.

"Then, you look me in the eye and tell me you don't love me anymore. Tell me that and I'll leave you alone. But you're gonna have to say it out loud and to my face, Tessie. That's the only way I'll ever let you go," he said.

She couldn't believe what she was hearing. Of all the nerve! Who did he think he was? She was never going to speak those words and put that weapon in his hands.

"You can't order me around. You're not my husband. You never will be. As soon as I can, I'll take Sam back to my *bruder*'s farm. I won't be working here and, except at church, we won't be seeing you anymore," she said.

His eyes clouded with pain, and he shook his head. He opened his mouth, as if he was about to say something, but he didn't get the chance.

A small gasp caused them to turn simultaneously. Sam stood in the doorway, holding his red lunch box with both hands. Lovina must have just dropped him off. Tessa had no idea how much of their conversation he'd overheard. From his wide, uncertain eyes and trembling chin, he'd heard plenty.

Without a word, the boy dropped his lunch box, then whirled around and ran into the kitchen.

"Sam!" Tessa called after him, but he scrambled out the back door.

She hurried after him, but he was way too fast. Flinging the screen door wide, she raced out into the alley just as Sam disappeared around the corner. By the time she got to the end of the lane, he was gone. For several minutes, she called to him, jogging up and down the street looking for him, to no avail.

She turned and found Caleb right behind her.

"Did you see which way he went?" he asked. He had been searching, too.

"*Ne*, I don't know where he is. He's never run away from me like this. I know he's upset, Caleb. But... I... I'm sorry I said those things to you. Sam loves you, and I know he wouldn't like it if he couldn't see you anymore. But I won't be with a man who doesn't love me. I can't accept your pity."

His jaw went slack, and he stared at her in surprise. "Tessa, who said I pity you? Who said I don't love you?"

She shook her head emphatically. "Please don't pretend. Not right now. I've got to find Sam. He's too young to be running around town on his own. He could get hurt or...or anything."

She heard the panic in her own voice, and her mind went wild with all the bad things she imagined could happen to her son. Her fear must have shown on her face, because Caleb reached out and squeezed her shoulder.

"You're right. We can wait. Don't worry. We'll find him," he said.

His reassuring smile gave her comfort, and she realized she'd come to rely on this man. Even though she'd hurt him, he'd given her a job. He'd been kind and protective. And look how she'd repaid him. It only reconfirmed that she didn't deserve such a good man as him.

As soon as she found Sam, she would swallow her

pride and send word to her brother to come and pick her and Sam up along with all their few possessions and move them back to his farm. She'd never be fully independent again, nor would she ever marry. It wasn't ideal. It wasn't what she wanted. But at least they'd be safe from men like Bryce and Glen. She'd put aside her haughtiness and focus on the joy of raising her son. That would have to be enough for her. And Caleb could move on with his life and marry a better woman than her.

It was the right thing for her to do. Wasn't it? Of course, it was! So, why did she feel so rotten inside?

Three hours of searching and still no Sam. Caleb glanced at the fading sunlight. It would be dark soon. Thankfully, it was summer and warm enough for the boy to be outside all night. But a four-year-old should never be left to roam around on his own.

Where could he be? They'd scoured the streets and asked everyone they met if they'd seen the child. They'd paused at the Amish soap works and bakery to explain the problem. Word had soon spread, and the Amish came out in droves to search. When the *Englisch* heard about the problem, they stepped up to help, too. Even Bryce Jackson had rallied his friends to comb the back roads circling the edge of town. Without being asked, the police set up checkpoints heading outside town, just in case someone tried to steal Sam. But Caleb didn't tell Tessa about that, as he figured she was filled with enough worry already.

Now, Caleb led the way down the stairs from her apartment. Over the past few hours, they'd returned twice, just in case Sam came home. They'd gone to Caleb's farm and the diner, too. Sam seemed to have disappeared into thin air.

Caleb would have suggested splitting up to cover more ground, but he didn't think Tessa was in any mental condition to be on her own right now. Her fear was palpable, and he couldn't blame her. Riverton was a fairly safe place to live and raise a *familye*. That was one reason he loved it here. This was the place where he'd hoped to marry one day and raise his own kids. With a population of around five thousand, everyone knew everyone else, including the Amish. But now, Caleb was concerned. He loved Sam like his own. For Tessa's sake, he didn't express his own apprehensions. She needed him to be strong right now. But later, once they'd found Sam safe and sound, Caleb was determined to convince Tessa they belonged together.

As he reached the bottom landing, Caleb looked up. Tessa was right behind him, in obvious distress. Her breathing came rather fast and uneven, and her face was drawn with worry. Though she gripped the railing as she descended the stairs, she missed a step. Caleb shot out an arm to save her from taking a bad fall.

"Are you okay?" he asked as he steadied her.

She wouldn't meet his eyes but nodded as she joined him on solid ground. He longed to tug her into his arms and whisper words of love and encouragement. To comfort her. But he knew she would never accept that from him.

She pulled away and stepped back.

"Where could he be?" she murmured to herself, her voice filled with tears.

"Don't worry. I know we're going to find him safe," Caleb said.

She gasped. "Look!"

He turned and saw a light on in the diner. Tessa was already running toward the door. Caleb followed hot on her heels. They'd left the back unlocked, just in case Sam returned. Maybe the boy was here. Maybe...

"Doris!" Tessa cried as the older woman met them at the door.

"Has there been any sign of him?" Doris asked, her eyes filled with unease.

"*Ne*, nothing yet," Tessa said, her shoulders sagging with disappointment.

"What are you doing here, *Mamm*? You should be *heemet* resting," Caleb said.

"Humph!" Doris reached to pull Tessa into her arms for a tight hug. "You poor dear. I'm not working, but I'm not going to sit at *heemet* worrying while all of you are out searching. I figured I could wait here in case Sam returns. I've been watching out the window to see him if he goes up to your apartment. But there's been no sign of him."

"*Ach, danke* for watching out for him." Tessa spoke half-heartedly, her eyes crinkled with anxiety and fatigue.

Doris gently smoothed a strand of golden hair back from Tessa's face and tucked it beneath her white prayer *kapp*. "Of course. You and Sam are like *familye* to me. I'm so sorry you have to go through this. It's every *mudder*'s worst nightmare, worrying about her child. What on earth made Sam run away in the first place?"

Tessa looked away. Caleb knew what she must be thinking. The angst and remorse were etched across her face. She feared Sam had overheard their entire conversation. It was bad enough the boy had witnessed them arguing, but to hear that he wouldn't be coming to the diner anymore was enough to set him off. Children needed stability in their lives. They needed to feel loved and secure.

Tessa needed the same things. In fact, after what she'd been through, Caleb figured she deserved it more than ever.

In the main dining room, she gazed out the window, her eyes searching the dark street. "My poor little boy. He's out there somewhere, alone and frightened. He would have come *heemet* by now. Something's wrong. I feel it in my bones."

"Let's go back out," Caleb said.

She nodded, and off they went. It was in the early hours of the morning, when the sun was barely peeking over the eastern mountains, that they returned to the restaurant. Tessa was tired and badly in need of rest. Her nerves were frayed, and she wasn't thinking clearly. And when Doris reported there still wasn't any news of Sam, Tessa finally broke down. It nearly shattered Caleb's heart anew to watch her weep openly on Doris's shoulder.

"My little boy. I can't even be a *gut mudder* to him," Tessa cried.

"There, there," Doris soothed. "That's not true. You're the best *mudder* that child could ever have. You're all he needs. We'll say another prayer and exercise our faith."

The woman glanced at Caleb, her gaze urging him to offer a vocal prayer on their behalf. Realizing he was the patriarch in the room, Caleb did just that. He thanked *Gott* for all their blessings, then beseeched Him to protect Sam and the searchers and help them find the boy soon. And when he finished, Tessa sniffed and wiped her eyes on her apron.

"*Danke*, Caleb," she said.

"It's amazing how *gut* children are at concealing themselves. They have an uncanny way of hiding where they can't be found." Doris patted Tessa's arm in a loving fashion.

"Doris! That's it!" Tessa exclaimed.

"Huh? What do you mean? What's it?" Doris asked.

Tessa whirled on Caleb, a tight smile curving her lips. The first smile he'd seen on her in several days.

"An idea just occurred to me," she said. "It might be nothing, but I think I know where Sam may have gone to hide. But we're going to need a flashlight."

Caleb blinked, not asking questions. He simply did as she asked and retrieved the requested item.

Doris bid them farewell. "*Gott* be with you. Bring our boy *heemet* safe."

As he helped Tessa climb up into his buggy, Caleb was glad he'd kept his road horse out all night. As soon as he could, he'd reward the animal with a nice rubdown inside his barn and an extra portion of grain.

"So, where are we headed?" he asked as he directed the animal down Main Street.

"Your place," Tessa said.

He gazed at her for several moments, his mind filled with questions. They'd already checked the barn and surrounding outbuildings hours earlier when they'd stopped off to quickly feed his livestock and see if Sam was hiding there. They'd found nothing, so Caleb was confused as to why Tessa thought Sam might be there now. But he didn't question her motives. They were out of ideas. He'd try anything if it brought them success. And for the first time in a long time, he let his faith in *Gott* and his trust in this woman be his guide. Nothing else mattered but finding Sam safe and sound. And afterward, he was going to have a long chat with Tessa, whether she liked it or not.

Chapter Fourteen

An urgency built within Tessa as she sat inside Caleb's buggy. The early-morning sunlight spread its faint glow across the green fields and enhanced the dark shadows. She caught the shimmer of moisture on the alfalfa growing in Caleb's fields. No doubt the warm summer sun would soon dissipate the dew. But right now, the cool early-morning air embraced her quaking body. She barely felt the chill. Her skin prickled with anticipation as they passed down Main Street and turned into the long drive leading to Caleb's farmhouse.

The horse trotted at full speed, but not fast enough for Tessa. Her little boy had been out alone in the dark, all night long. For five years, Tessa had kept the truth of Sam's birth a secret from everyone but *Gott*. She'd hoped to protect Sam. And she'd tried to forgive the man who'd hurt her and forget it ever happened. She wanted to move forward. To make a fresh start. But she wouldn't marry a man because he pitied her.

Looking at Caleb, she noticed his harsh profile was

set with determination, his jaw locked hard as granite. Without asking, she knew he felt as urgent as she did. They had to find Sam.

"Haw!" He slapped the leather leads against the horse's rump, pushing the animal to move even faster.

Finally, he pulled the buggy to a stop just in front of his barn. Tessa didn't wait for him to come around and help her down. Gripping the flashlight, she bolted from the vehicle like it was on fire and dashed toward the south field.

"Where are you going?" Caleb called after her.

She barely glanced his way, seeing his look of surprise. No doubt he expected her to go to the barn again. But not this time.

"To the abandoned water well," she yelled over her shoulder.

He ran after her, asking no more questions. Tessa remembered Doris telling her that her father-in-law had boarded up the mouth of the well, but Caleb's siblings and their friends had pulled the boards off years ago, when they were kids.

Together, they sprinted at full speed, jumping over clumps of dirt and grass in their path. In spite of her head start, Caleb arrived at the well before her and looked down. Tessa got there moments later and did likewise, staring into the black maw. She shone the beam of the flashlight down the thirty-foot hole, then gasped when she saw her son's pale, tearstained face gleaming up at them.

"Sam! *Ach*, Sam!" she cried, almost overwhelmed with relief.

"Mammi!" he called back, his voice hoarse, as if he'd been screaming for hours.

"Sam, are you *allrecht*? Are you injured?" Caleb asked.

"Ja, my wrist hurts awful bad," he said.

"How did you get down into the shaft?" Tessa asked.

"I used the old rope tied to the well and shimmied down, but it broke. I fell, and that's how I hurt my wrist," he said.

"It could be broken. If that's the case, he can't climb up without help," Caleb said.

That was Tessa's thought exactly. As she shone the light around her son, she could see that he was sitting on a wooden board. It looked like one of the timbers that had been nailed across the mouth of the well by Caleb's grandfather over twenty years earlier. Somehow, the board had been dropped into the well and wedged against the sides to provide a platform for Sam to sit on. If not for that slim piece of wood, her son would fall to the bottom of the well…a thought that absolutely terrified Tessa. And even worse, she had no idea how long the board might hold her son's weight.

"Look! The well is not stable." Caleb pointed at the wall of the shaft. Through the dark shadows, Tessa could see places where the rock wall had caved in.

"How do we get him out?" she asked, her voice trembling.

"I don't want him to fall any farther. There's no telling how long that board he's sitting on will hold him up. The shaft is thirty feet deep. Right now, it looks like he's only about fifteen feet down. If he falls deeper, he could be badly hurt. I know you're anxious, Tessa, but listen to me." He cupped her face with his hands and stared directly into her eyes, seizing her attention. "Stay here with Sam, but don't do anything more than encourage him to remain very still. Keep him quiet while I go to the barn and get a new rope and one of my horses. Then I'll climb down to Sam and we'll pull him up. *Allrecht?*"

She nodded, captured by his gentle but confident voice. He turned and sprinted back toward the barn. Watching him go, a feeling of absolute calm washed over her. And in that moment, she realized she had confidence in this man. Not once had he betrayed her or let her down. He'd been there for her whenever she needed him the most.

She trusted him completely.

Turning, she gazed down at her son. He lifted his good hand toward her.

"*Mammi!* Get me out," he sobbed.

"We will, *liebchen*. Hold on," she soothed in her most loving voice. "But listen to me now. You've got to stay very still for a few minutes more. Caleb has gone to get a rope. You've got to be strong and brave just a little while longer. Can you do that for me, sweetums?"

Cradling his injured hand against his chest, he wiped his eyes with his good hand and nodded. She kept talking to him in her gentlest voice, making sure he could see her and know that she was there. And in her heart, she realized *Gott* had always been there for her, too. Comforting and offering her strength. During her darkest moments, the Lord had never abandoned her. Not once.

The sun rose in the eastern sky, spraying light and

warmth across the field. It couldn't have been more than ten or fifteen minutes as they waited for Caleb to return, but it seemed like an eternity. Tessa heard the thud of heavy hooves and looked up, surprised to see him riding the back of his largest draft horse as the animal galloped toward her. When he reached the well, Caleb slid off the gray's back and handed her the reins.

"*Ach*, hold Pete still for me. When I give you the signal, you're going to slowly pull Sam and me up," Caleb said.

She nodded, clutching the leather firmly in her hands. She stroked Pete's velvet muzzle and watched in silence as Caleb tied one end of a strong rappelling rope to the harness. She remembered going hiking in the mountains with him and the other youth of their congregation when they were kids. Under the supervision of adults, they'd rappelled short distances down a mountain cliff. It had been a fun and challenging activity, and she'd felt happy and carefree. But back then, she wasn't a worried mother and no one's life had been in danger.

Now, Caleb wore a rappelling harness around his legs and waist and a pair of leather gloves on his hands. Using a figure-eight belay device and a locking carabiner for a secure point of anchor, he stepped up onto the rock lip of the well. Pieces of dilapidated stone dropped to the ground, attesting to the severe decay of the wall.

Facing her, Caleb nodded, and she pulled on Pete's reins, leading the big horse forward until the rope went taut.

"*Ach*, hold it steady right there. I'll tell you when to pull. Just move really slow," Caleb called.

"Got it," she said.

He smiled with reassurance and then did something she didn't expect. He winked, and she barely caught his whisper.

"Don't worry. It's gonna be okay," he said.

Leaning back, he fed the rope through the belay device as he gradually walked himself down until he disappeared from view. She knew he would rappel along the shaft until he reached Sam.

She longed to run over to the mouth of the well and look down but couldn't abandon her post. She had to hold Pete steady. Both Sam's and Caleb's lives depended on her.

Minutes ticked by, and she knew Caleb must be positioning himself so he could hold Sam securely before she could pull them up. She waited patiently, speaking gently to the horse, sending a prayer heavenward.

"Okay, pull us up!" came Caleb's faint request.

Though he must have yelled to her, his words sounded watery since they came from a hole in the ground. But Tessa didn't have to be told twice.

Moving gradually, she tugged on Pete's halter and led him forward. The rope went tight as it bore Caleb and Sam's weight. Standing at nineteen hands high and weighing in at around fifteen hundred pounds, Pete's muscles bunched and flexed as he pulled hard.

The rub of the rope sounded harsh against the mouth of the well, sawing against the stones as the man and child were lifted from the dark hole. Finally, Tessa saw them, but she resisted the urge to run to her son until Caleb could maneuver them both safely onto solid ground. As he did so, the rotted boards that made up the pulley to lower the bucket into the well gave way. They plunged into the shaft, and she heard rocks pounding downward as more of the decayed wall collapsed inward.

"Sam!" she cried, running to her son.

Caleb stood cradling the boy in his arms, holding him snug against his chest. Tessa threw her arms around them both and buried her face against Sam's neck as she let go of her inhibitions and wept openly.

"Mammi!" Sam cried, holding her head with his good arm.

She kissed his face again and again. "Are you okay?"

He showed a half smile. "I am now."

She released a happy but slightly hysterical laugh. "Don't you ever run away like that again, young man. Promise me?"

Sam nodded. "I promise, *Mammi*. I won't ever hide in there again."

"That's right, because I'm going to fill that well in next week so no one else can ever be hurt there again," Caleb said.

Sam's expression turned rather severe as he looked at his mom. "But I want to know something, too. Are you gonna make us leave the diner and move back to *Onkel* Wayne's farm?"

She nodded. *"Ja*, that is my plan. Why is it so important to you that we stay at the diner?"

"Well, all the other kids at church have *vadders*. But I don't. For the longest time, I just had *Onkel* Wayne. I love him and he's nice and stuff, but he's not my dad. At the diner, I have Caleb. And I want to know, who is my real *daed*?"

Tessa stared at him, too shocked to respond at first. She opened her mouth to answer, but Caleb didn't give her the chance.

"I am. I'm your *daed*, Sam," he said.

Sam looked at the man and blinked, his eyes round with disbelief and a heavy dose of pleasure. "Honest? You're my *daed*?"

"*Ja*, I am." Caleb locked his jaw hard and gazed steadily at Tessa, as if he dared her to deny it.

Sam flung his good arm around Caleb's neck and hugged him tight. "*Ach, Daedi!* I knew it was you. I just knew it."

Tessa didn't know what to say. How she longed for it to be true. How she wished she and Caleb had married years earlier and now shared this sweet little boy together. Caleb was making things so easy for her. From the wide smile that spread across Sam's face, he liked this news. It would be so easy to pretend that Caleb was really Sam's daddy. After all, that was what Tessa wanted most in this world. But she couldn't lie. Not when she and Caleb weren't married and never would be.

Over the top of Sam's head, Caleb spoke in an unmistakable whisper.

"Let it be, Tessie," he said.

But how could she? The tenets of her faith demanded she be honest in all things. Eventually, Sam would have to be told the truth. But not right now. Later on, when he was old enough to understand.

"Are…are you hurt anywhere else? Do you feel any pain?" she asked her son.

"*Ne*, just in my wrist. I can't bend it," Sam said.

She looked at his hand where it lay pressed immobile against his small chest. Both the hand and wrist were quite swollen and bruised.

"I think it's broken," Caleb said. "We should get him over to the hospital right now so he can be checked out for internal injuries. Can you remove the harness from Pete? He can graze here in the field. It's fenced, so he won't get out while we're gone. I think it's most important to take care of Sam first," Caleb said.

"*Ja*, of course." She quickly did as he asked, then joined him as he carried her son toward the house.

As she walked beside Caleb, a feeling of deep and abiding gratitude filled her heart. They could call off the searches now. Her son had been found and safely recovered from the well. Thanks to Caleb.

Three days later, Tessa laid a pile of blankets inside a cardboard box and closed the flaps. Lifting the box, she set it on top of several others in the living room of her apartment. Tomorrow morning, Wayne was coming with his wagon to load up her and Sam and their few possessions. Knowing her leaving the diner would put Caleb in a bind, she'd asked Wilbur and Esther Schwartz, the retired couple from Pennsylvania, if they would be willing to fill in until Caleb could hire someone permanently. Under the circumstances, they'd agreed.

Walking down the hallway, she peered into Sam's room. Evening shadows gathered around his bed. He lay on his back, his face turned toward the window, where a faint summer breeze ruffled the curtains. Since it was still quite warm, he had only a sheet pulled over him. At the hospital, they'd x-rayed his wrist and found that it was definitely broken, and he'd received a cast to keep it immobile while it healed. Other than a few bruises and a new fear of dark tunnels, he seemed whole and unhurt. Tessa had promised to leave a light on in his room.

Next week, she was going to consult with a specialist to see how she might help him get over the horror of being alone in a dark hole for hours until they found him. And maybe she'd talk to the specialist about what had happened to her in Denver, too. It might help both of them heal from the trauma they'd each suffered. But she had absolute confidence they could overcome these problems in time. She couldn't explain it, but she felt different somehow. Like she was free and whole. That she could overcome anything. She'd finally handed her guilt and pain over to the Lord, and, for the first time in years, she felt absolutely free. And she had Caleb to thank for it all.

While she'd been in the hospital with her son, Caleb had left them long enough to call off the searches and notify the police that Sam had been found. Two officers had come to the hospital to check it out and take her statement.

Sam had stayed there overnight, just for observation. Wayne and Grace had come to visit, expressing their love and support. Wayne had even told her he would build a small house behind his home where she and Sam could live. The thought of being with her family, yet having her own place, brought a flood of tears to Tessa's eyes. But leaving the diner would be more than difficult. She couldn't explain that, either, but she'd come to love her work there. Helping Caleb and Doris gave her a sense of purpose. She'd even miss her little apartment.

A low knock sounded on the door, drawing her out of her musings. She stepped over to the portal and leaned close.

"Who is it?" she asked.

"It's Caleb. Can I *komm* in, please?"

Caleb! He was here.

Taking a deep breath to settle her nerves, she opened the door. He'd been leaning one arm against the threshold and quickly stood, whisking his straw hat off his head and holding it before his chest. A slight smile curved his handsome mouth. He was clean-shaven and had combed his hair. She couldn't help noticing he wore his pristine white shirt, black vest and broadfall pants. Glancing down, she saw the dirt had been brushed off his boots, too. He still looked quite plain, but she caught the subtle differences. He only wore these clothes to church or for special occasions.

"*Hallo*, Caleb," she said, wondering why he was all dressed up.

"Hi, Tessa. I was wondering if we could talk for a few minutes."

She opened the door wider and stepped back. "Of course. *Komm* in."

He did so, closing the door behind him. "Is Sam here?"

"*Ja*, I put him to bed about thirty minutes ago. It

seems he's worn-out from his ordeal. I've never seen him sleep so much," she said.

"That's *gut*. He needs rest. I'm sure he'll be fine and racing around again in a couple of days."

"*Ja*, I'm sure he will." She sat on the edge of a chair and indicated he should sit on the sofa.

He did so, his gaze sweeping across the room. When he saw the boxes piled against the far wall, his head jerked toward her, his forehead curved in a frown. "Are you moving?"

She forced herself to meet his gaze. "I… I am. I think it's for the best, for Sam and me."

His frown deepened, and she hurried on.

"I spoke to Wilbur Schwartz this morning, and he said he and Esther could work at the diner until you find a replacement for me. I… I'm sorry, Caleb. I've thought a lot about this. I'm moving back to Wayne's farm in the morning. I know you told Sam that you're his *daed*, but we both know that isn't true. I so appreciate you giving me a job. I learned so much, and it was a great experience for Sam and me to be on our own. But…after what happened, I think I should put some distance between us. For Sam's sake."

He sat back and took a deep inhale, releasing it ever so slowly, as if he was gathering his thoughts. "I've been thinking, too, and I believe I have a better solution for all of us."

She perked up at that. "Oh? And what is it?"

"I'd like you and Sam to move into the house on my farm and live there with me and *Mamm*. I want you both to be safe and happy there."

She gasped. "We can't do that, Caleb. It wouldn't be proper."

"It would if you married me. That's what I still want," he said.

Her heart stopped, then beat madly within her chest. "Caleb, I can't..."

He held up a hand, cutting her off. "Wait and hear me out, Tessie. When you came *heemet* from Denver all those years ago and broke up with me, I thought my world had ended. Then you gave birth to Sam out of wedlock. For years, I've watched and waited for his *vadder* to show up and take you both away. But he never came. I was so confused, wondering what happened. Wondering how a man could ignore his own beautiful child and a woman as amazing and lovely as you."

Tears burned her eyes, and she brushed them away, but they just returned, running down her cheeks. "I... I know, Caleb. But I couldn't tell you. Don't you see? I barely knew him and he hurt me more than I can say. I had to protect Sam, no matter what."

He sat forward, leaning his elbows on his knees as he searched her face earnestly. "I understand, Tess. Truly I do. And I don't blame you, sweetheart. But I also was angry and hurt. For the longest time, I couldn't figure out why you would abandon me and the promises we made to each other without some logical explanation. Now, I finally know the truth. With everything you've gone through, you've been a stand-up woman all these years, loving and raising your *sohn* with kindness, patience and faith. Even when people gossiped about you, not once did you falter. I know you've felt guilty for what happened."

She looked down, and tears dripped onto her folded hands. "I never should have gone without you. But what happened at the party wasn't my fault. I know that now, but it took a long time for me to realize it."

"I've felt guilty, too," he said. "For letting you down. For not being there when you needed me the most. But I want you to know, you did nothing wrong. I don't pity you, Tessa. Not at all. I admire you. More than any person I've ever met. Your faith and inner strength amaze me. I think that's why I love you so much. You're the most marvelous woman I know."

She looked up and released a sad little sigh. "Do you really mean that, Caleb? Because if you do, I can't tell you what that means to me."

He nodded. "I do mean it. With all my heart. And after five years, I have to ask you a most important question." He paused for a moment and took a deep breath before letting it go. "Haven't we both suffered enough? I don't want to take away any of your independence or freedom, Tessie. I want to be a team with you and make our decisions together, with love and compassion for one another. I just want to love you and share our lives. Together."

"You…you really love me? You're not just saying that?" she asked, her voice filled with a mixture of hope and disbelief. Her heart was beating like a bass drum. She couldn't believe what she was hearing.

Or could she?

"I do. I love you so very much. And I think it's time for us to forgive one another and to forgive ourselves, too. *Gott* wouldn't want us to mire our lives in sadness forever. That's why He sent His only begotten Son. To atone for our sins. To offer forgiveness and healing so we can move forward and have joy. It's what we both believe in, isn't it?"

She blinked. "*Ja*, but… I don't know what to say. It is what I believe, but…"

"But what? Is *Gott*'s forgiveness for everyone else but not for us?" he asked. "That's not right, Tessie. The atonement of Jesus Christ is for you and me, too. And I believe it's time for us to move forward and be happy. We have our whole lives ahead of us. We're still young and strong. It's time for us to marry and create a *familye* together. Sam needs that, too. I'm his *daed*. In my heart, I'll always be his *daed*."

He knelt before her on both knees, and she widened her eyes in awe as he took her hand in his, looking up at her with absolute love and hope shining in his eyes.

"Tessa Miller, I would be so honored if you would marry me and make me the happiest man in the world."

Her mouth went slack, and she stared at him with dripping eyes. She couldn't stop the flow of tears to save her life. He didn't mean it, did he? She couldn't believe this was happening. Not to her. Not when it was the fondest desire of her heart. And yet, she was tired of rejecting him. Tired of being alone and fighting against the love she'd always had for him. And just like that, she finally let go of her doubts and fears. As she gazed at his beloved face, all her misgivings evaporated. Nothing seemed to matter at that moment but him and their love. But what about tomorrow? She couldn't forget what had happened to her. It was part of who she was. But she realized it was time to put it aside, now. To finally let it go.

"Say *ja*, *Mammi*! Say *ja*!"

She turned and saw Sam standing in the doorway, dressed in his jammies. Their voices must have awoken him. The white cast on his hand and wrist stood out like a flag of truce. A glow of happiness and anticipation emanated from his face. How could she refuse Caleb when both she and Sam loved him so much? How could she deny the very thing she wanted most in life? Caleb and a life together as a real *familye* had been her greatest dream.

"*Ach*, Caleb! I love you, too. I always have." The words burst from her lips like a dam breaking free.

And suddenly, she was in his arms. He held her close, kissing her lips, her cheeks, her eyes. And somewhere during that moment, she heard her son's gleeful laughter. Caleb picked up the boy, and he joined them in a three-way hug. Finally, they grew quiet and she looked up at Caleb, the tip of her nose touching his.

"I need to hear you say it out loud, Tessie. Will you marry me?" He spoke ever so softly, his warm breath grazing her lips.

"*Ja*, I will, Caleb. I'll marry you and love you till the end of time," she whispered back.

He kissed her again, and out of her peripheral vision, she saw Sam cover his eyes with his hands.

"Yuck! Are you gonna do this kissy stuff all the time now?" the boy asked, his happy voice telling her that he really didn't mind at all.

Caleb chuckled and opened his eyes, but he didn't stop kissing Tessa as he spoke against her lips. "*Ja*, we are. I love your *mamm* and plan to kiss her as often as I can, so get used to it."

Tessa laughed, too, overwhelmed with joy and basking in Caleb's declaration of love. This was all she needed to hear. She couldn't believe her life was now going to be filled with kisses, hugs and love. So much love. Because *Gott* had wrought such a blessing in their lives. The blessing of forgiveness. And she was not about to fight against it anymore. How could she? This was exactly what she wanted the most.

* * * * *

*If you enjoyed this Secret Amish Babies story,
be sure to pick up the previous book in
Leigh Bale's miniseries,*
The Midwife's Christmas Wish,
available now from Love Inspired!

Dear Reader,

Have you ever encountered someone who made a poor decision that ended up costing them dearly? Maybe their poor judgment impacted your life as well. Perhaps their decision wasn't really bad per se, but it was inconsistent with the dictates of reason or the ordinary rules of prudence and it led to a folly of high consequence.

In this story, Tessa Miller made a poor choice by going with a friend to a party where she didn't know anyone else. In the process, she was taken advantage of, and the outcome completely changed her life. Her choice wasn't necessarily bad, but she put herself in a situation she could no longer control. Her reckless choice ultimately led to her having a child out of wedlock and destroyed her relationship with the man she loved.

Thanks to the Atonement of Jesus Christ, all our lapses in judgment can be forgiven. Through the power of repentance, we each may receive God's healing balm and find joy as we serve Him. There is no foolish act, no traumatic event, no broken heart or ill health that cannot be healed by the power of our Savior's sacrifice.

I hope you enjoy reading this story, and I invite you to visit my website at www.LeighBale.com to learn more about my books.

May you find peace in the Lord's words!
Leigh Bale

WE HOPE YOU ENJOYED
THIS BOOK FROM

LOVE INSPIRED
INSPIRATIONAL ROMANCE

Uplifting stories of faith, forgiveness and hope.

Fall in love with stories where faith helps
guide you through life's challenges, and discover
the promise of a new beginning.

6 NEW BOOKS AVAILABLE EVERY MONTH!

LIHALO2021

COMING NEXT MONTH FROM
Love Inspired

IN LOVE WITH THE AMISH NANNY
by Rebecca Kertz

Still grieving her fiancé's death, Katie Mast is not interested in finding a new husband—even if the matchmaker believes widower Micah Bontrager and his three children are perfect for her. But when Katie agrees to nanny the little ones, could this arrangement lead to a life—and love—she never thought could exist again?

THEIR MAKE-BELIEVE MATCH
by Jackie Stef

Irrepressible Sadie Stolzfus refuses to wed someone who doesn't understand her. To avoid an arranged marriage, she finds the perfect pretend beau in handsome but heartbroken Isaac Hostettler. Spending time with Sadie helps Isaac avoid matchmaking pressure—and handle a difficult loss. But can they really be sure their convenient courtship isn't the real thing?

THE COWBOY'S JOURNEY HOME
K-9 Companions • by Linda Goodnight

Medically discharged from the military, Yates Trudeau and his ex-military dog, Justice, return to the family ranch vowing to make amends—and keep his prognosis hidden. Only civilian life means facing reporter Laurel Maxwell, the woman he left behind but never forgot. When she learns the truth, will she risk her heart for an uncertain future?

CLAIMING HER TEXAS FAMILY
Cowboys of Diamondback Ranch • by Jolene Navarro

After her marriage publicly falls apart, single mom Abigail Dixon has nowhere to go—except the family she thinks abandoned her as a child. Not ready to confront the past, Abigail keeps her identity a secret from everyone but handsome sheriff Hudson Menchaca. Can he reunite a broken family...without losing his heart?

THE SECRET BETWEEN THEM
Widow's Peak Creek • by Susanne Dietze

In her mother's hometown, Harper Price is sure she'll finally learn about the grandfather and father she never knew. But that means working with local lawyer and single dad Joel Morgan. Winning his and his daughter's trust is Harper's first challenge...but not her last as her quest reveals shocking truths.

EMBRACING HIS PAST
by Christina Miller

Stunned to learn he has an adult son, widower Harrison Mitchell uproots his life and moves to Natchez, Mississippi, to find him. But Harrison's hit with another surprise: his new boss, Anise Armstrong, is his son's adoptive mother. Now he must prove he deserves to be a father...and possibly a husband.

LOOK FOR THESE AND OTHER LOVE INSPIRED BOOKS WHEREVER BOOKS ARE SOLD, INCLUDING MOST BOOKSTORES, SUPERMARKETS, DISCOUNT STORES AND DRUGSTORES.

Get 4 FREE REWARDS!

We'll send you 2 FREE Books plus 2 FREE Mystery Gifts.

FREE Value Over $20

Both the **Love Inspired®** and **Love Inspired®** Suspense series feature compelling novels filled with inspirational romance, faith, forgiveness, and hope.

YES! Please send me 2 FREE novels from the Love Inspired or Love Inspired Suspense series and my 2 FREE gifts (gifts are worth about $10 retail). After receiving them, if I don't wish to receive any more books, I can return the shipping statement marked "cancel." If I don't cancel, I will receive 6 brand-new Love Inspired Larger-Print books or Love Inspired Suspense Larger-Print books every month and be billed just $5.99 each in the U.S. or $6.24 each in Canada. That is a savings of at least 17% off the cover price. It's quite a bargain! Shipping and handling is just 50¢ per book in the U.S. and $1.25 per book in Canada.* I understand that accepting the 2 free books and gifts places me under no obligation to buy anything. I can always return a shipment and cancel at any time. The free books and gifts are mine to keep no matter what I decide.

Choose one: ☐ **Love Inspired**
Larger-Print
(122/322 IDN GNWC)

☐ **Love Inspired Suspense**
Larger-Print
(107/307 IDN GNWN)

Name (please print)

Address   Apt. #

City   State/Province   Zip/Postal Code

Email: Please check this box ☐ if you would like to receive newsletters and promotional emails from Harlequin Enterprises ULC and its affiliates. You can unsubscribe anytime.

Mail to the Harlequin Reader Service:
IN U.S.A.: P.O. Box 1341, Buffalo, NY 14240-8531
IN CANADA: P.O. Box 603, Fort Erie, Ontario L2A 5X3

Want to try 2 free books from another series? Call 1-800-873-8635 or visit www.ReaderService.com.

---

*Terms and prices subject to change without notice. Prices do not include sales taxes, which will be charged (if applicable) based on your state or country of residence. Canadian residents will be charged applicable taxes. Offer not valid in Quebec. This offer is limited to one order per household. Books received may not be as shown. Not valid for current subscribers to the Love Inspired or Love Inspired Suspense series. All orders subject to approval. Credit or debit balances in a customer's account(s) may be offset by any other outstanding balance owed by or to the customer. Please allow 4 to 6 weeks for delivery. Offer available while quantities last.

Your Privacy—Your information is being collected by Harlequin Enterprises ULC, operating as Harlequin Reader Service. For a complete summary of the information we collect, how we use this information and to whom it is disclosed, please visit our privacy notice located at corporate.harlequin.com/privacy-notice. From time to time we may also exchange your personal information with reputable third parties. If you wish to opt out of this sharing of your personal information, please visit readerservice.com/consumerschoice or call 1-800-873-8635. **Notice to California Residents**—Under California law, you have specific rights to control and access your data. For more information on these rights and how to exercise them, visit corporate.harlequin.com/california-privacy.

LIRLIS22

SPECIAL EXCERPT FROM

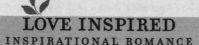

LOVE INSPIRED
INSPIRATIONAL ROMANCE

*Cowboy and veteran Yates Trudeau returns home to his
family ranch bruised and battered and carrying a
life-changing secret. When he bumps into
Laurel Maxwell, the girl he left behind, she might just
set him on the path to healing that his body—and his
heart—so desperately needs...*

Keep reading for a sneak peek at
The Cowboy's Journey Home,
part of the Sundown Valley series by
New York Times *bestselling author Linda Goodnight.*

Had he really come to the woods before going to the
ranch house? She had a feeling she was right and that
he had. She wondered why—another habit of journalists.
She needed to know everything, especially motives.

Yates's gaze seemed glued to her face, and she fought
off a blush that would let him know he still affected her
on some unwanted, visceral level. People say you always
remember your first love. Yates had been her first and
only.

She'd spent the better part of a year waiting to hear
from him and another year getting over him.

Now here he was in the flesh, stirring up old memories.
At least for her.

The annoying blush deepened. Laurel turned her
attention toward the children and the dog. With a smiling

Justice in the center, they formed a circle of petting hands and eager chatter.

"Those aren't all your kids, are they?"

A small pain pinched inside her chest. "Sunday school class." To turn the focus away from her, she asked, "Was he really a military dog? Like a bomb or drug sniffer?"

"Explosives."

"Did something happen to him? Why'd he retire?"

Yates's face, already closed, tightened. "Stuff happens. Soldiers retire. Look, I should go. Enjoy your picnic."

With a snappy military about-face, he started to walk away.

"Yates, wait."

He paused, gazing back over his shoulder.

"After you get settled, come by the *Times* office. I'd love to interview you and the dog for the paper." She put her fingers up in air quotes. "'Hometown Hero Returns' would make a great feature."

"No interview. We're civilians now. Nothing heroic about that." Turning away, he gave a soft whistle. "Justice, come."

Before she could say more, Yates and his dog disappeared into the foliage.

Don't miss
The Cowboy's Journey Home *by Linda Goodnight,*
available August 2022
wherever Love Inspired books and ebooks are sold.

LoveInspired.com

Copyright © 2022 by Linda Goodnight

LIEXP0622